The Assertive Woman

A N D

Other Anomalies

The Assertive Woman

AND

Other Anomalies

MARSHA DRAKE

BETHANY HOUSE PUBLISHERS
MINNEAPOLIS, MINNESOTA 55438
A Division of Bethany Fellowship, Inc.

Published by Bethany House Publishers
A Division of Bethany Fellowship, Inc.
6820 Auto Club Road, Minneapolis, Minnesota 55438

Printed in the United States of America

Library of Congress Cataloging-in-Publication Data

Drake, Marsha.
    The assertive woman and other anomalies / Marsha Drake.
        p. cm.
    1. Women—Conduct of life—Fiction. I. Title.
PS3554.R233A9   1989   813'.54—dc19   88–33338
ISBN 1-55661-019-X   CIP

Dedicated to:

my grandfather, Pal

Table of Contents

From October to August
In the house in the shadow of the Chief

1 / Heartache

"And Deborah, a prophetess, the wife of Lappidoth, she judged Israel at that time."[1]

Mr. Kleaver clutched his chest. "Martha, help me to my office."

Wide-eyed with horror, I stared at my balding boss. "It's all right, Mr. Kleaver." Answering the call of duty, I hefted my five-foot frame under his right arm. "Probably nothing more than another slight heart attack," I counseled. "I'll have an ambulance here in no time."

"Ginnny!" I shouted in a hoarse whisper to the grocery checker in the next check-out lane. "Call an ambulance!"

"Oh my!" Ginny's eyes screamed shock under her yellow hair. "Oh!" Staring, she stood still.

"Good grief," I complained, sagging under Mr. Kleaver's weight. Hauling him along down the aisles, I prayed under my breath: "Lord! Help! Keep him breathing, please, God, because Ginny will never come to her senses in time to telephone anyone."

"Oh, Martha," Mr. Kleaver groaned.

"Just hang on, Mr. Kleaver." I hefted him a little higher and hurried down a back aisle, through the swinging doors marked "For Employees Only," and over to a stack of boxes where I deposited him heavily. "Just stay here while I call someone for you," I comforted, loosening his tie and collar. "Try to keep breathing, and be calm."

"Jimmy!" I yelled at the empty storeroom. "Jimmy! Jimmy! Where are you?"

Silence.

"Oooh," Mr. Kleaver sighed. His face turned ash-white. Beads of perspiration rolled down his forehead.

Racing back through the swinging doors, I screeched, "Jimmy!"

"Coming! I called 'em, Martha!" Ginny raced down the aisle toward me. "They're on their way!"

"Where is Jimmy, Ginny?" I demanded.

"Is he sick too?" Her blue eyes mirrored my anguish.

Suddenly sirens screamed the ambulance's arrival.

"Excuse me, Ginny," I threw over my shoulder, racing back to Mr. Kleaver.

After the attendants had safely loaded Mr. Kleaver into the ambulance, I turned my attention store-ward.

"Ginny, stop crying. Where is Jimmy?"

"I don't know . . . Oh, Martha, what are we going to do? Is Mr. Kleaver going to die?"

"Ginny," I commanded, "stop sniveling!"

She burst into fresh sobs.

"Look, Ginny, I am sorry. Okay?" I put my arm around her shoulders reassuringly. "We have all been under a terrific strain."

She daubed her mascara, smearing it across her right cheek. "But what are we going to do?"

"Simple." I smiled to assure her of my confident manner in emergency situations. "I, as Assistant Manager, will take over for our employer, and everything will come up roses." I waved my hand in the direction of the entire supermarket and noticed chaos.

"Ginny, please go back to your cash register." Shoving her gently, I patted her back at the same time. "Just tell the customers the emergency is over."

Wiping her eyes again, she timidly suggested, "Should I turn up the music?"

"Good idea, Ginny. Now you're *thinking*."

"In the meantime, I'll find Jimmy. Where can a stock boy be at 11:30 in the morning?"

"Asleep! Jimmy, how can you be asleep in the morning?" I loomed over my errant stock boy and glared menacingly.

"What's the matter, Mrs. Christian?" He rubbed his eyes and yawned.

"Why are you sleeping?" Placing my hands on my hips, I used my most authoritative tone.

"Huh?"

"Huh?"

"What?"

"Jimmy, don't *ever* let me catch you sleeping on the job again. Now get up off the sawdust and stock some shelves or something." I whirled away in disgust.

"Wait a minute, Mrs. Christian." Suddenly Jimmy leaped to life. "Don't tell Mr. Kleaver." He hung his head.

"I don't have to tell Mr. Kleaver, Jimmy. I am in charge now. You are looking at your new boss."

No sooner was the store humming along, when an attractive, willowy thin woman with snapping dark eyes and raven black hair approached me in checkout number one.

"Are you the check-out person in charge?" Her voice hit my ears like melted butter.

"Uh, yes," I responded, dropping a can.

"I believe I bought these at your store." With a perfectly manicured set of fingers, she held out a brown paper bag.

"What seems to be the problem?" I smiled cheerfully.

"Maggots," she responded. "I saved one for you to see." She whisked open the sack and pulled out a clear, plastic bag containing one piece of candy and two worms.

I looked into the eyes of a timeless woman whose face would never age, and crumbled before her gaze. "Would you like a different box of candy?"

Just then Jimmy appeared at my elbow. "Mrs. Christian," he interrupted, "I heard what the lady just said, and I don't think the worms will hurt her. They mostly like to live in the nuts . . . ."

"Jimmy, go to your room—I mean the stockroom, please." I faced my accuser again.

"Of course, I will give you your money back. I'm so sorry for any inconvenience this may have caused you." Fumbling, I opened the cash drawer and fingered the bills. "How much did you pay?"

"I purchased four boxes. Don't you know how much your candy costs?" She stood easily in her low-heeled shoes.

"Certainly," I replied brightly. "Of course!" Dipping my hands into the money, I pulled some out and hoped for the best. "Would you happen to have your sales slip?"

"No." She held out a dainty hand and waited.

Crossing her palm with a few bills and some silver, I felt sick. "At Kleaver's Meats and Merchandise we always aim to please," I replied politely.

"Thank you," she stated succinctly. Then she and her fashionable skirt floated out of the store.

Somewhere in my head I felt like a little gray mouse had just met a sleek, black cat ready to pounce.

"Are you all right, Martha?" Ginny's voice broke through my reverie.

"Fine. Let's close early today."

After closing the store, counting cash, and visiting my ailing boss in the hospital, I arrived home to cook dinner. As soon as my ears were inside, I heard the sounds of life—teenage life.

"Now what are they up to?" I grumbled, climbing the stairs to the kitchen.

"Get out! Get out! I told you to keep that dumb dog off my bed, J.J.!"

Mentally I noted, *Joe is home.* I waited for John Jr.'s response.

"Oh, yeah?" The sounds of running feet and a machine gun. "Take that!" I heard water squirting at great force, hitting walls.

"Missed me!" Middle son, Joe, hollered. "Wait till I get my water balloon!"

"Wait till I get both of you!" I shrieked above the din.
Silence.

Marching back to their bedroom, I squared my shoulders for battle. "All right, you two. Why hasn't anybody peeled the potatoes, and why aren't you doing your homework, and what is the dog doing in the house and on Joe's bed, John Jr.?"

"Slow down, Mom!" J.J., my seventeen-year-old interjected.

"Yeah, Mom. You're going to give yourself a heart attack," chimed Joe.

"What do you know about heart attacks, Joe!" I retorted.

"John Jr., get Specimen out of this house and into the dog house where he belongs!" I snapped.

"No problem, Mom," they chorused. "Just don't get into a flap about it."

"If you two think you can join forces and do me in, you've got another think coming!"

Looking at each other, my two oldest sons thought better of saying more and decided to pout instead.

Ignoring their snarling faces, I inquired politely, "Where is your brother George?"

"In his room, probably," John Jr. stated without interest.

"Probably?" I nearly blasted them with my thoughts about their lack of attention to baby-sitting their twelve-year-old brother, but didn't.

"He's mostly in his room playing with his dumb pig Ben," Joe explained, shoving his hands into his pockets.

"Well, at least he's not watching television. That's good." I glanced around their room and noticed Specimen slobbering on a bone.

"John Jr. . . ."

"*John!* I am seventeen now, you know." He puffed his chest in manly pride.

"Yes." I nodded my head affirmatively. "I know."

"We are supposed to reason; not shout," he continued.

"Yes, I know that, J.J., but I would like to point out that Specimen, although a lovely animal as dogs go, is still a labrador-mutt mix who needed a bath six months ago and who has a house of his own to live in."

"So?" His blue eyes challenged my right to live.

"So, if you ever hope to drive the car again, take him outside to his own home and make him comfortable *there*."

"Good idea!" He brightened. "Do you have any errands for

me to run today?" He gathered his canine companion in one swoop.

"Maybe later." I smiled good-naturedly, "After Specimen is safely sleeping—in his house." I took a deep breath. "How about a hug for your aging mother, guys?"

"Awww, Mom . . ."

After giving my almost-men a few compliments in regard to their respective heights and growth of feet, I departed for George's room.

"Hey, big guy, how ya doin'?"

George sat on the floor of his room surrounded by nails and boards. "Fine, Mom. Hey, look at this!"

I stared at a piece of wood riddled with nails. "You would have made a good cobbler," I joked.

"Yeah, what's that, Mom?" He bent over his shoes.

"It's a person who makes shoes."

"Oh, well, Ben doesn't wear shoes, but that's a good thought, Mom." He furrowed his brow as he dug around for a suitable nail.

"Ever think of doing this in the basement?" I approached the subject gently.

"Yeah, but Ben doesn't live down there. He lives with me in my room."

"Oh."

"Just a few more changes." He chomped his tongue in concentration.

"Looks good, George—what you're building."

"Yeah. It's a spaceship."

Walking toward the kitchen to start supper, I wondered why Ben wouldn't need shoes, but would need a spaceship. "I could lose my mind easily around here . . ."

As soon as dinner was over and the kids were off to their various pursuits—J.J. writing a letter to his moved-away-girlfriend, Babs; Joe poring over a fighter pilot book; George teaching guinea pig Ben how to play "chess"—I sat down with husband John to get his reactions to the day's events.

"How about a cup of coffee, John?" I hollered from the kitchen.

"No thanks. I'm off caffeine today," he said from behind his newspaper.

"That was simple," I replied, sitting next to him on the sofa.

Laying the paper down, he said, "Martha, what is it?"

"Why? Because I asked you if you wanted a cup of coffee?"

"No," he smiled uneasily, "because I know your look."

"What look?" My innocent expression covered my apprehensions at what he would say about me taking over Kleaver's Meats and Merchandise without consulting him.

"That look that tells me you have gone and jumped into something, and now you want my approval, or at least my lack of disapproval."

"Hmm, well, that's a little complicated, John, but I do have something to discuss with you." I kissed him lightly on the cheek.

He looked at me and waited.

"Yes, well, Mr. Kleaver had a heart attack at work today . . ." Seeing his concern, I plunged right ahead, "And I had to take over."

"Good. I thought this was going to be a major issue." He picked up his paper.

"Permanently." I rested my case.

"What do you mean, *permanently*?" The paper went down again.

"John, you remember Deborah, the fourth judge who delivered Israel, don't you? Why, her victory paralleled the rule of the Egyptian pharaoh, Ramases III. He was the last great pharaoh, you know." I leaned back comfortably. "I am going to deliver Kleaver's from financial ruin just like Deborah." I glanced at him out of the corner of my eye.

"Can't somebody else deliver the groceries?" John yawned.

"I am going to run the business, John. There is no one else."

Furrowing his brow, he adjusted his glasses, picked up his paper and replied, "I will pray for you, Martha."

"Thanks, John! I knew I could count on you." I gave him a hug, patted his paper, and departed to do my hair for the next working day.

The week went well, and by Saturday, I had the store running like an oiled hinge.

Sunday morning I was up and dressed before the rest of the family. "Something sure smells good in the kitchen, Martha." John followed his nose to the oven. "Ah, my favorite—apple-crumb coffee cake." His eyes beamed.

"Yes, dear," I grinned. "Are the kids up?"

"They're up, but not moving. I'll go prod them a bit."

We made it to church on time. "Thanks, Martha," John whispered approvingly as we sat down in the pew. "I hate to be late."

"I know." I smiled happily. "Lord, this is great," I prayed. "Smooth sailing. I love it!"

Settling myself on the soft seat, I glanced around the church. "Hi, Jean!" I waved and whispered, nodding my head in friendship.

My dearest buddy of fifteen years, Jean Marks, flashed a quick grin before she bowed her head to pray.

Then I spied neatly coiffured, raven black hair two rows over to my left. "It couldn't be." Shivering shocks twisted my stomach into knots. Tearing my gaze from the back of the mystery lady's head, I tried to concentrate as we stood to sing the first hymn.

Concentration evaded me. I heard nothing, including the sermon, for the next hour. Over and over in my mind the scene of the "maggot lady" replayed itself. "Worms! I sold worms!" I thought in desperation. "What if she comes over to say hello?"

" . . . and so, it gives me *great pleasure*," Pastor Jim Jacobson's deep voice rang into my thoughts, "to present a very special lady—one who comes to us from Mapletown with her glowing achievements going on before her." Pastor Jim gestured toward the congregation.

"Andrea Gray, will you come forward, please?"

"Oh my!" Dizziness swept through my system, leaving me with cold chills. "It's her." Slumping in my seat, I looked around guiltily as she made her way to the front of the church.

When she turned to face the people, I covered my face with my right hand and looked down.

"Feeling all right, Martha?" John said, watching me crumple into a heap.

Four weeks passed before I actually encountered Andrea Gray. Standing in the church vestibule, I had deliberately turned my back when John made his way through the Sunday morning crowd to greet her. Then it happened.

"Martha," John beamed, "I don't believe you've met Andy."

"Oh!" I jumped as he touched my elbow from behind.

"Hello, Martha!" Andrea's voice coursed through my veins. "John has told me so much about you."

Since no hole in the floor opened to provide emergency service to the basement, I turned and faced the woman I'd sold worms to. Looking straight at her perfect shoes, I intoned, "Oh."

When I lifted my quivering gaze to meet her steady, almost black eyes, I knew that she knew that I knew who she was.

She and I played at small talk as John welcomed visitors to our church.

By the time we arrived home, I had an awful headache. "John, I'm going to take a nap. I don't feel well."

While I rested, my eyes ran around the room and counted cracks in the woodwork. Since I couldn't sleep, I tried to read. Then I heard John's voice on the telephone.

"Hello!" His bass voice rang out.

Straining my ears, I struggled to hear the conversation. *Probably has something to do with his Sunday school class. John is so conscientious about his young people's class."* Goodnaturedly, I listened.

Nothing.

Curiosity caused me to tilt one ear toward the door. I heard him speaking in muffled tones.

Finally he hung up.

Then I dozed off to sleep.

The following morning, I felt groggy as I groped around the kitchen looking for something to cook.

"What's for breakfast, Mom?" George flew into the kitchen, straight to the refrigerator, where he grabbed Ben's customary morning carrot.

"I don't know, George," I replied from the cupboard.

"Okay, Mom!" Joe stomped in the kitchen, grabbed some plates, and slapped them on the table. "Dad said I have to help you, so here I am, but it's J.J.'s turn; not mine!"

"Yes, Joe." Mechanically I moved out of his way. "Excuse me."

Hurrying down the hall to the bathroom, I sought sanctuary. The door slammed shut as I arrived. "Anybody in there?" I queried politely.

"I'm shaving, Mom. What do you want?" The door spoke— using John Jr.'s voice.

"Are you going to be long?" I asked.

"I just got in here, Mom! Joe hogs the place all the time . . ." His voice trailed off as I trekked back to the kitchen.

"Think I'll make soft-boiled eggs. John likes that," I muttered to myself.

"Joe!" I woke a bit when I saw toast burning in the toaster under the cupboard. "You are steaming up the sugar!"

"What's the problem, Martha?" John appeared.

"No problem," I answered evenly. "What would you like for breakfast?"

"Poached eggs on toast."

"Certainly," I said through thin lips.

He kissed me lightly on the cheek. "George up?"

"*I'm* not up."

"I'll go get him. Doesn't he set the table or something?"

"Or something," I replied under my breath.

John departed for the back of the house.

"Where is the pan to poach the eggs?" I said to the oven drawer. "The special coated one—so I won't have to spend hours scrubbing it at midnight tonight."

Something told me to look in the fridge. "Of course." I shoved the door shut in disgust. "It's full of chicken soup. Who was on dish duty last night?"

Buddy, the bird, flew over, resting his parakeet feet in my hair.

"Not now, Buddy. I'm cooking." Putting my hand on top of my head, I felt for his fluffy blue body.

"Okay, fella. I don't know who left you out, but you're going back to the safety of your cage."

"Peep, good Buddy-bird-bird," he replied as I carried him on my finger back to the living room.

Cautiously I approached his swinging cage. "I know this isn't your favorite spot, Buddy, but I have to be at work early today, and you could be bird meat for Specimen if I—"

"Squawk! Scree! Cheep!" He bolted and flew for the drape tops.

"Oh, Buddy." I walked after him. "Not now."

Tilting one eye toward me, he replied, "Good Buddy!"

"J.J.!" I yelled. "Will you please get Buddy!"

No reply.

"John Jr.!" I hollered louder.

"What!" he screeched back in adolescent baritone.

"What are you doing?" I lowered my voice slightly.

"Shaving!" He screamed louder.

"Still?" My shoulders sagged. "Never mind, I'll get him my-self."

Back at the fridge, I discovered somebody bought grade *B* eggs.

Shoving aside what I'd recently read about cancer and grade *B* eggs, I dropped them into boiling water.

Finally the family arrived at the table.

"Eggs are a touch hard in the center, Martha," commented John.

"I have to leave right now," John Jr. stated.

"Why?" I asked.

"No reason."

"You want to go to school *early*?" I stared at my offspring.

"What's wrong with that?" His blue eyes snapped.

I looked at John.

He nodded affirmatively.

"See you after school, J.J." I made a mental note to watch him more closely.

"How come the eggs are all sloppy?" Joe spoke.

"Somebody stored chicken soup in the pan I cook eggs in," I replied triumphantly.

"J.J. did it. I saw him." George shoved his egg to the left off his toast and stuck out his upper lip. "Yuk."

"George, please. Not now." I pleaded for cooperation.

"If I eat this, it's going to make my appendix scar hurt."

"See you later, Martha. I'm late." John grabbed a mouthful of orange juice and headed for the door.

"Can I have a ride, Dad?" Joe sparkled with enthusiasm.

"If you hurry."

"All right, George, it's you and me now. What will you eat for breakfast?"

"Ice cream."

"George," I coddled, "it's been months since you had your operation. Your appendix is not there. You will not get another stomachache if you eat. Don't you understand that?"

He stared down at his plate.

"Okay, George," I smiled convincingly, "how about some cereal?"

"Can I pick it out?"

"Yes—if you drink two glasses of milk. You still need to gain some weight back, you know."

When I arrived home from the store that night, weariness washed over me as I entered the house. "That's funny," I commented to myself, "no noise."

I listened. "Hmmm, where is Specimen?" I walked back outside. "Why, I don't believe it! Specimen is asleep next to his house, and his leash is on!"

Hurrying back into the house, and ominous foreboding forced me to stumble as I raced up the stairs. Afraid to call out, I peeked into the living room first.

"Surprise! Surprise!" The room leaped into life and filled with people. "Happy birthday!"

Mouth open, I stood there staring at smiling faces. Then I started to cry.

"Wow, Mom!" George appeared at my side. "Isn't this great? And wait till you see the cake!"

"Where is your father?" I asked, still in shock.

"He's out in the kitchen with Mrs. Gray." He stuffed a double-chocolate cookie into his mouth.

"George, limit those. Remember your braces . . ."

"Happy birthday, honey." John suddenly stood beside me.

On the surface it seemed to be an extraordinary event. Underneath my skin, it spelled disaster in my relationship with John. Unable to understand Andrea Gray's connection with the whole event, I felt certain she was at the other end of John's previous muffled telephone conversation. "Why is *she* in *my* kitchen?" I wondered.

"Happy birthday, Martha." Andrea arrived from my kitchen and stood next to my husband. Every raven-colored hair in place, she stood serene in her newest fashion.

Late that night, after the rest of the family lay sleeping, I did something I hadn't done in years. Tiptoeing out to the kitchen telephone, I dialed surreptitiously, waiting for the phone to ring.

"Hello?" The familiar voice sounded sleepy.

"I'm sorry I am calling so late . . ."

"Are you all right, Martha?"

In the face of adversity, I did not face Andrea Gray. I did not tell my husband how much it hurt to have my age of forty announced in front of everybody, while he stood next to timeless, vivacious Andy. Aware of every wrinkle, seeing my husband admire a younger woman, denying my vulnerability, I called home.

"Mother?"

2 / *Dirge*

"Awake, awake, Deborah; awake, awake, sing a song!"[2]

"Psst! John!" Shifting nervously on my seat next to John in the third pew, I gently jabbed him with my pointer finger and coughed.

A small snore escaped from my husband's slack mouth.

"John, please!" I hissed quietly. Glancing uneasily around, I leaned over and whispered in his ear. "What will Andrea think?"

Without moving his head, one eye popped open and rolled around aimlessly.

Closing in for the kill, I dropped my hymnbook on the floor, shoved next to John, and elbowed him hard in the ribs.

Both his eyes flew open. "Amen!" he intoned to a hushed congregation.

Pastor Jim Jacobson raised his head which had bowed for prayer, shot a glance in our direction, and said, "Let us pray."

Hot waves of embarrassment swept up my neck into my hairline, and I shivered. The pastoral prayer escaped my attention as my thoughts reverted to my late-night phone conversation with my mother.

Standing in the kitchen, the night chill had caused my voice to quaver. "Mother?"

"Are you all right, Martha?" The well-modulated tone of my mother's familiar voice seemed connected to my tear ducts.

24

"Yes, Mom," I sniffed.

"Sweetheart, I tried to phone earlier to wish you a happy birthday, but the line was busy every time. I was worried . . ."

"Oh, that's fine, Mom!" I shoved a smile on my face and lied. "That's why I'm calling now. I knew you'd want to wish me a happy birthday!"

"Is everything all right with the children?"

"Sure, just great." I wiped my nose with the back of my hand. "Ben is building a spaceship for George, and John Jr. misses Babs a lot, and Joe is weight-lifting this year . . ."

"Did you say Ben?"

"Ben?" My mother knew me too well. Stress often caused me to reverse words or thoughts.

Forcing a chuckle, I responded. "*George* is building a space vehicle for Ben." I rubbed my eyes with the thumb and forefinger of my right hand. "Don't worry, Mom. Everything is fine. I'm cold and should get back to bed now."

Climbing back into bed, I dismissed my upset as overwork and lack of rest . . .

"Martha." John's shoulder gently pressed against mine. "Sleeping?" he chided, nodding his head toward the front of the church.

"Praying, John. Just praying," I fibbed as I arranged myself uncomfortably to pass the offering plate. I wondered when the pastoral prayer had ended and the collection had begun.

I was not ready for the next part.

"Andrea Gray, will you come forward, please?" Mr. Wesley Ward stood tall at the front of the congregation.

A reverential hush seemed to sweep the sanctuary as the tall, slim, strong Andrea Gray floated her way forward.

Unable to help myself, I drank in her every move, her fashionable dress, her perfect hair. Her master's degree seemed etched upon her face as she smiled confidently.

"At a special board meeting last evening, Mrs. Gray was unanimously voted in as our new Sunday School Superintendent."

"Why didn't I hear about this, John?" I whispered in surprise.

John didn't answer. He nodded his head approvingly toward the front of the church.

Guiltily I folded my hands in my lap.

"Thank you, Mr. Ward." Her voice swept across the quiet sanctuary and into my anxious ears where it hit like sticky syrup. "As the new superintendent, I have a few changes to make . . ."

John leaned forward in rapt attention.

I noted, *John never listens to me that attentively.*

"We will be doing things differently this year . . ."

I clued out until I heard our names.

"Mr. Christian will be working in close conjunction with the overall picture, and I'm assigning Mrs. Christian to be in charge of snack time."

"John," I whispered loudly, "did you hear that? I haven't got time to be in charge of cookies and juice! I have thirty preschoolers! I'm lucky if they stay in the room, let alone—"

John didn't hear a word I said, but the lady next to him did, and she glared at me. I sank lower into my seat.

Then I wondered, *What does "close conjunction" mean?*

By the time Andrea Gray's announcements were over, the congregation was clapping, and indigestion rocked my stomach.

John gazed straight ahead.

As soon as the last note of the final hymn trailed into infinity, I poked John and said audibly, "Let's split."

"Split?" His eyebrows lifted high on his forehead.

"I have a splitting headache, John. Can we go home now?"

"In a minute, Martha." His eyes scanned the scattering group of people, then riveted themselves to a raven black head that glided effortlessly through the swarm which politely shoved toward the outside exit. "Ah, there she is," he remarked to himself.

"Who?" I suicidally inquired.

"Andrea," he responded absent-mindedly. Without a backward glance in my direction, he melted into the crowd.

"John!" I uttered a cry of frustration. "Where are you going?"

"See you outside, Martha," he called back through three people.

George appeared at my elbow. "What kind of cookies are you

going to get, Mom? I like double-chocolate-fudge with extra frosting best."

"Where is Joe?" I demanded, ignoring his request.

"I dunno. Want me to find him?"

"Find him!"

"What's wrong with you?" He crinkled his face in disgust. "I didn't do anything so you don't have to yell at *me!*" His parting shot rang through several families who turned and stared at me and my offspring. Lamely, I tried smiling.

People are so cold at church, I thought while waiting in line to go outside.

By the time my face finally felt crisp November air, I had decided nothing could be gained by feeling upset. *After all*, I comforted myself, *what does Andrea Gray have that I haven't got besides superior education, slim good looks, and youth?*

Pastor Jim's handshake felt phony. "How are you today, Martha?" His deep baritone rang like a noisy gong.

"Fine." I spoke off the top of my head. "How are you?"

"Why, thank you for asking, Martha! As a matter of fact, I've been experiencing a bit of back pain. If you could pray . . ."

I heard no more. I saw, however, John Jr. in the company of a teenage-type female. Instantly I noticed her long blond hair and mermaid figure.

Marching right over, I said, "Hi, J.J.!"

Both adolescent faces flushed cherry pink.

"Oh, hi, Mom," J.J. responded stiffly.

"Hi," I repeated, looking meaningfully at the mermaid.

She giggled and flashed sea-blue eyes at my son.

"Oh!" John Jr. stammered nervously. "This is . . . Laura!"

"Hello, Laura," I replied, sizing her up and rating her a zero on a mother's scale of wholesome-goodness-for-her-son.

She flashed her dimples at my eldest.

"We're leaving soon, J.J.," I advised. "I'll meet you at the car."

"Sure, Mom," he responded without seeing me leave.

The car welcomed me like a quiet cave. I steamed and waited.

"Oh, here you are, Martha." John hopped into the driver's seat.

"Where did you expect me to be?" I answered frostily.

"You could have been polite, Martha." His eyebrows pulled together most unbecomingly. "Andy has invited us over for dinner tonight to discuss the new fall Sunday school program—"

"*Andy?*" I interrupted. "You call her Andy? Sounds pretty masculine to me." I crossed my arms in front of me and looked out my car window.

"Where are the kids?" John ignored my sarcasm.

"They'll be along soon, I guess." I eyed my pink nail polish.

"What about dinner?" John's direct question threw me off guard.

"What about it?" I said saucily.

"Hi, Mom! Hi, Dad!" George shouted through my car window.

"Just get in, George," I responded.

"Sure, Mom!" My youngest son yanked open a back car door and jumped inside. "Did you see Laura?"

"Who's *Laura?*" Joe leaped in the other side and shoved over against George.

"Stop pushing, Joe!" George shouted.

Joe's muscular fifteen-year-old arms shot out and put George in a head lock.

"Mom!" George screamed.

"Joe, stop it," John said, glancing into the rear-view mirror.

"He's just a baby." Joe suddenly let go. "Aren't you a baaaby!"

"Joe!" I whirled around in my seat. "Your father told you to stop it, so *quit!*"

"What's wrong with you, Mom?" Joe's brown eyes feigned surprise.

"There'll be something wrong with you in about two minutes, Joe, if you don't settle down," I warned, turning around again.

"Where is John Jr.?" I fumed impatiently.

John looked in the back seat. "George, want to take a look for J.J.?"

"Sure, Dad!" He threw open the door and raced off to look for his brother.

"Want me to look too, Dad?" Joe asked hopefully.

"No!" I answered for both of us.

John started the engine. "They'll be along in a minute. Thanks, son."

I peeked at John out of the corner of my left eye. I could see irritation. "So!" I began brightly, "what did you think of the sermon?"

John put the car in gear. "I'll look in the parking lot."

I'd overstepped my bounds and knew it.

Once we'd collected our three sons, silence held our family in check on the way home.

Like an armed camp, we drove into our driveway, spilled out of the car into the house, and retreated to various rooms and activities.

"Think I'll bake a cake," I muttered to myself, reaching for a favorite cookbook. "Chocolate. George likes chocolate."

"I'm going to Jeff's house to lift weights, Mom," Joe informed me on his way out the door.

"Be home in time for dinner, Joe," I replied, pulling out flour, eggs, and sugar.

"See ya later, Mom," John Jr. said on his way past me.

"Where are you going?" I inquired.

"Out."

"Out? What do you mean out?" I turned to face my six-foot son, raising my eyebrows in blue-alert position.

"It's okay, Mom." John Jr. reached out and patted the top of my head. "Laura, you know, the girl you met at church? I'm going to her house to do some homework." He stepped back, smiled, and headed for the door.

"Wait!" I commanded. "Your homework is supposed to be done by Saturday afternoon. That's the rule . . ."

He smiled easily and flashed the grin that got me married to John. "Slip of the tongue, Mom. I meant *Bible* homework—for next week's Sunday school class. Mrs. Gray is teaching the high school class now."

"When did *that* happen?"

"This morning at church. You were probably dozing off. You

know, like you nap after supper sometimes. We learned about it in biology."

Outclassed, I let him go. "Will you be home for dinner?"

White teeth sparkled underneath twinkling blue eyes—John's blue eyes—"I'll call you, Mom."

Once I heard the door slam, I fought back tears. "Everything is happening too fast, Lord," I whispered. "John Jr. is almost grown—he graduates this year—I am getting older, and John . . ." Quickly scraping the devil's food cake batter into a prepared pan, I popped it into the oven and went looking for John.

"John?" I spoke to an empty living room. "And where is George, come to think of it?"

Suddenly I felt sorry for my behavior in the car. "Probably nothing to worry about. John is always patient with me. I know he'll understand when I tell him I am worried that he likes Andrea better than me, and it will be all over with in a hurry."

Unable to locate John or George in the house, I went outside. "That's ridiculous," I announced to a pruned rose bush. "I can't tell John I'm afraid he no longer finds me attractive! What will he think? People tell that kind of thing to a psychiatrist!"

I walked around the house to the backyard. The silence of the moment soothed me. "I love autumn air," I mused aloud.

"What? Did you say something?" My neighbor's face appeared over her fence top.

"I was looking at the Chief!" I countered.

"Oh." She smiled knowingly. "Oh."

"The mountain!" I pointed to the gigantic monolith that occupied the horizon—just twenty stones' throws from our backyard. Ambling over to the fence, I waxed friendly. "I'm sorry. You've been here at least a month and I haven't been over with cookies, or even invited you over for coffee."

She walked down toward the end of their fence, pulling a rake along behind her.

I followed along on my side of the wooden-spiked barrier. "I work at Kleaver's Meats and Merchandise," I continued, "and I'm gone a lot."

"Oh," she responded.

"So, that's why I haven't gotten to know you, or that you haven't gotten to know me," I finished.

"Oh," she replied, leaning on her rake.

"Doing some raking, I see." I tried to initiate a new vein of conversation.

"Yes," she replied.

"Uh, huh," I answered accordingly.

She picked up her rake and adjusted the scarf covering her dark brown hair.

"I'm looking for my husband," I explained cheerfully.

"Oh," she responded, raking multi-colored leaves into a neat pile.

"Did you know that mountain isn't a mountain at all?" I offered cheerily. "It's a granite cliff!"

"Oh!" she said just before she disappeared into her garage.

"Oh," I repeated softly. "Oh, well, maybe she doesn't speak English or something. I'll have George deliver some chocolate cake later today. That's if I can *find* George!"

Trooping toward the front yard, I spied my husband and son George walking down the sidewalk toward our house. As soon as they got within earshot, I hollered, "Where have you been?"

"We went for a walk, Mom!"

"Oh," I replied. "It must be catching."

"What's catching, Martha?" John inquired.

"I'll explain it later, John. George, I'm baking a chocolate cake—"

"All *right*!" He shouted and whooped his way toward the back door. "I'll check on it for you!"

"Don't open the oven door!" I yelled as the back door slammed shut.

"Sorry, John, about before," I said simply, linking my arm in his.

"Me too," he announced, squeezing my arm. "Anything on your mind?"

"Why do you ask?" My tension erupted into flying things in my stomach.

"Maybe you've been working too hard at Kleaver's, Martha. You seem tired."

"Do I look tired?"

"A little." He grinned. "But I love those little wrinkles you're getting around your eyes."

Pain like a dagger shot through my system, forcing every hair to stand on end. "Yes. That's it, John. I am tired. Very tired." Turning on my heels, I headed for the back door.

John hurried ahead and held it open for me. Usually I loved that bit of attention. Today, however, it irritated me. I ducked under his arm and hurried inside.

"Martha." John's tone stopped me in my tracks. I knew what he was about to ask. "What about dinner at Andy's tonight?"

Caught, I couldn't move.

"Well?" The air hung heavy between us.

"I'm too tired, John." Without a backward glance, I fled into the kitchen.

What's wrong with me? I wondered, grabbing the cake out of the oven. *I don't usually treat John like that. It's immature, and rude to boot.*

John appeared at the kitchen door. "What shall I tell Andy?" he asked. I couldn't look at the hurt in his eyes.

"John, I am really not feeling well." I turned the cake onto a rack. "And the kids need dinner here, and I have a big day tomorrow." I squared my shoulders and faced him. "Can't you go without me?"

The telephone rang. Glad for the interruption, I seized the receiver. "Hello?"

A perfect voice replied, "Martha? This is Andrea Gray. May I speak to John, please?"

My pent-up fury would have powered a nuclear reactor. "Just a moment, please," I intoned like a switchboard operator. "It's for you, John."

His puzzled expression did not deter my wrath as I dumped icing sugar, cocoa, an egg, and some vanilla into a bowl.

"Oh, yes, Andy! Of course we would love to come, but Martha isn't feeling well . . ."

I glared at the mixing bowl and stirred furiously. Then I heard the straw that broke the camel's back.

"I guess I could come alone, if you feel it is that important,

Andy. No, I'm sure Martha won't mind."

He handed me the phone. "She wants to speak to you."

"Hello?" My cowardly tone sickened me.

"Martha, I am so sorry you're not well enough to come over tonight, but you must understand that I need John's opinion of everything, since he and I will be working in close conjunction on this project." She paused.

Instead of asking her just how close a conjunction she planned, I replied, "What was it you wanted to speak to me about, Andrea?"

A lilting laugh washed through the telephone lines. "Call me *Andy*, Martha. John does."

"I know," I sniped.

"I thought you could get cookies for us from Kleaver's Meats and Merchandise for our Sunday school morning snack time." She paused as a queen waiting to be served.

"What?" I squeaked.

"As a donation."

"I couldn't possibly, Andrea," I said unconvincingly.

"Perhaps you could discuss it with Mr. Kleaver. I am certain you wouldn't want to make this decision on your own."

She answered my arguments before I gave them. "But—"

"Just make sure you check the cookies," she cleared her throat for emphasis, "for freshness—if you know what I mean."

I knew what she meant—the maggots. Blackmail won where reason would have failed. "I'll see what I can do."

"I would like them for next Sunday, Martha. You pick the flavor."

Like a well-trained prisoner, I replaced the receiver carefully.

"Everything all right, Martha?" John inquired.

"Fine," I prevaricated.

No one came to dinner except George.

"Wow, Mom, this chicken is great! Where'd you get it?" George piled his plate high with fried wings.

"The freezer. It came in a box."

"Oh, well, they still taste great." With a huge bite in his mouth he mumbled, "How come there's no gravy?"

"Because it's frozen, George," I answered, picking the fried skin off my pieces of white meat. "Frozen box-chicken can't make gravy, and please don't ask me why."

"Why are you scraping off the skin? That's the best part!"

"To save calories, George."

He nodded his head, scrunched his brows, and salted his wing. "Where is everybody?"

"Dad is eating dinner at Mrs. Gray's, J.J. is eating at Laura's, and I haven't heard from Joe, who should have been here half an hour ago."

"Uh oh, he's gonna get it." George's blue eyes opened wide and stared at the double-fudge chocolate cake on the table. "Can I have cake now?"

"What about your vegetables?"

"They make my appendix scar hurt." His eyes dropped down in abject misery.

"George . . ."

"Anyway, Mom, it's like a big, fat, ugly earthworm crawling across my stomach and it itches too." He scratched his side a couple of times.

The basement door slammed. "Hi, Mom! I'm home!"

Wearily I filled Joe's plate with fried chicken, dressing, snow peas, and steamed potatoes. "Why are you late, Joe?"

He ran up the stairs two at a time. "You'll never believe it, Mom!" I didn't.

By the time John Jr. arrived, I was sitting in the living room with my feet up.

"So, Mom, how's it going?" John Jr. planted himself in an easy chair.

"What about Babs, J.J.?" I got right to the point.

"Babs?" He leaned back comfortably.

"Yes, *Babs*. You know, Barbara Murrey who stole your heart last year and whom you've been writing to for the last six months since she moved away and who—"

"I get the point, Mom." He stood up and walked toward the door.

"Well?"

"Well, Babs is there, and . . ."

" . . . Laura is here." I completed his sentence for him.

"That's type-A behavior, Mom. You could have a heart attack, you know."

He disappeared just before the sofa pillow that I threw hit its mark.

Chuckling, I retrieved the cushion, fluffed it, and replaced it on the couch. My well-worn Bible lay nearby on the end table. Picking up the book I said to myself, "Now, what was that I was reading about Deborah a couple of days ago?" I thumbed through the pages of Judges. "Deborah would be a good subject for our women's Bible study this year. Think I'll bring it up."

Settling myself on the end of the sofa, I read, "Awake, awake, Deborah . . . sing a song! Arise, Barak, and take away your captives, O son of Abinoam."[3]

"Nice," I commented, "but who was Abinoam?" I scanned the preceding page. "Now Deborah, a prophetess, the wife of Lappidoth . . ."[4]

The telephone rang. Hurrying to answer it I remarked, "Well, Abinoam wasn't Deborah's husband anyway."

"Hello?" I expected to hear John's voice saying he would be late.

"It's only me." In three words Jean identified herself and reestablished our friendship of fifteen years.

"Hi, Sis," I quipped. "I'm glad you called. I was thinking Deborah would be—"

"—a good subject for our Bible study." She finished my sentence for me.

"That's type-A behavior," I commented dryly.

"J.J.'s been picking on you again, I see," she said with a laugh.

"You and I understand each other so well, Jean. Why is that?"

"We speak in shorthand."

"Right." I agreed. "What do you want?"

"Just to say hello. The house is quiet."

"Here too. Where's Hub?"

"Out with the kids. John?"

"Andrea Gray's." I waited for her response to that one.

"Oops! Here they are. Talk to you later, Martha!" And she hung up.

By the time John Jr., Joe, and George were settled for the night, I began to worry. "Where is John?" Pacing back and forth across the living room, I glanced out at my favorite mountain, the Chief, and wished I hadn't met Andrea Gray. Why did I feel all thumbs and toes around her? She hadn't done anything to me. I should have been happy to help with the Sunday school.

"Good night, Buddy," I clucked to our blue-tailed parakeet. Covering his cage with a royal blue cloth, I felt old. "That's probably it. I am aging, and this is part of that."

Not long afterward, I lay in bed trying to sleep. Where was John?

Then I heard the back door close.

Like a guilty child caught reading in bed with a flashlight under the covers, I whipped off the light, covered myself to my nose, and closed my eyes.

"Martha?" Softly he spoke from our bedroom door.

My mouth sealed itself shut as my eyelids independently squeezed tighter together.

Quietly my husband moved through the back of the house, turning down the heat, shutting off lights. Then he disappeared into his den.

From my vantage point, I could hear every move he made. He was *singing*!

3 / Judging

"And she used to sit under the palm tree of Deborah between Ramah and Bethel in the hill country of Ephraim; and the sons of Israel came up to her for judgment."[5]

"George, will you take these cookies to the lady next door?"

"What lady?" His braces glinted in the December sunlight streaming through our kitchen window.

"The one who moved in next door a few months ago," I replied absent-mindedly, busily stuffing plastic containers with freshly baked gingerbread boys.

"Why do we have to give any away? You never make enough of them anyhow, and I—"

"I don't want to argue, George." Setting my mouth to firm resolve, I snatched a cookie from my hungry adolescent boy who was home from school with a mild cold.

"And affix this red bow on the top, please."

"Is this a Christmas present, Mom?" Cheerfully he mashed the crimson bowknot onto the carefully wrapped package.

"No, it's because you ate all the chocolate cake the last time I made one, and I didn't have a chance—"

"Let's not argue, okay, Mom?" George pushed his glasses higher on his nose, adjusted his rumpled jeans, and grinned.

"I don't know our neighbor's name, George, but I know she is at home today. You can recognize her easily. She says 'oh' a lot."

"What do I get?" He eyed a cooling cookie.

"A *cookie*." I grabbed his arm stretching toward the counter. "When you *return*!"

By the time he returned, I'd safely stashed the gingerbread boys in the deep freeze, cleaned up the kitchen, and had settled myself on the sofa. "Now! Back to the Book of Judges, Deborah, and good old Abinoam—whoever he is."

"Mom! Mom!" George roared into the living room.

"George, I am trying to read," I responded, ruffling pages in my Bible. "Your cookie is on a plate in the kitchen."

"Never mind that, Mom!" George scratched his scar. "Mrs. O has something strange in her backyard!" Taking me by the arm, he hauled me over to our big picture window.

Glancing out, my eyes fixed on a strangely shaped object—obviously under construction behind Mrs. O's house.

"What do you think it is, Mom?" His voice rose in excitement. "A spaceship?"

"Don't be ridiculous, George. It looks like a playhouse to me." Closing the drapes, I pulled his nose away from the window. "Why didn't you ask Mrs. O?" My eyes opened wide. "Why are we calling her Mrs. *O*?"

"Because she says 'oh' all the time."

"Oh," I commented, cuffing him playfully on the chin. "Your gingerbread man awaits you."

Like a flash of lightning, George hit the kitchen.

Meanwhile, my curiosity about the identity of Abinoam drove me to my Bible dictionary. "Hmm," I remarked, running my finger along the printed page, "this is interesting—'Abinoam: father of kindness, the father of Barak' (Judges 4:6; 5:11)."[6]

"That's nice," I mumbled, putting the dictionary down and leafing through my dogeared Bible to Judges, chapter four.

"Now Deborah, a prophetess, the wife of Lappidoth, was judging Israel at that time. And she used to sit under the palm tree of Deborah between Ramah and Bethel in the hill country of Ephraim; and the sons of Israel came up to her for judgment . . ."

"Ah-ha!" I exclaimed. "At least somebody listened to her!"

" . . . Now she sent and summoned Barak the son of Abinoam from Kedesh-naphtali, and said to him, 'Behold, the Lord, the God of Israel, has commanded, "Go and march to Mount Tabor, and take with you ten thousand men from the sons of Naphtali and from the sons of Zebulun . . ." ' "[7]

"Mom?" George's voice boomed into my reading.

"What?"

"There was only one gingerbread man." The hungry eye was back.

"George!" Still in shock from his appearing in the midst of Mount Tabor, I yelled first, then repeated calmly, "George, there are no more. Please build a spaceship for Ben."

He narrowed his eyes suspiciously, scrutinized my face for intent of malice, then answered, "Sure."

Alone again, I remarked, "Hmm, Barak who?"

"Hi, Mom! We're home!" Joe and J.J.'s voices rang through the house.

"How did it get to be 3:30?" I asked myself. "Hi, guys!" I hollered back in a friendly fashion.

"I love days off," I muttered, heading toward the kitchen.

After dinner, I approached John as he sat reading the newspaper. "Who was Abinoam?"

The newsprint rustled slightly; then a voice from afar said, "Not sure, Martha."

"He was Barak's father," I advised.

The paper resumed normal reading stance—stationary and quiet.

"Who was Barak?" Gently I poked the paper in the middle.

"I guess we're going to talk now," John replied flatly, his face replacing the newsprint I'd been reading.

"Excuse me for interrupting, dear. It's just that you're a better Bible scholar than I am, and I'm wondering who Barak was." I smiled amiably.

Removing his reading glasses, my spouse smoothed his thinning hair, and concentrated. "I'm afraid to ask how this began."

Checking out the twinkle in his soft blue eyes, I continued with confidence. "Last week I was looking up Deborah because I think she would be a good subject for our women's Bible study this year."

He nodded, listening carefully. It was one of the qualities I loved most about John—his ability to listen well to everyone— not just to me.

"I came across Abinoam in a Bible dictionary, and I found out he was the father of Barak, and now I'm wondering what you know about Barak. You taught Judges last year in Sunday school."

Slowly he smiled, put down his newspaper, and replied, "My memory of it is a bit sketchy, Martha, not precise like yours."

"Is that an insult? Get serious, John," I teased.

With a mischievous glint in his eye he began, "Barak, the son of Abinoam, from Kedesh-naphtali, was summoned by the prophetess Deborah to muster the tribes of Israel and lead them into battle against Sisera (the commander in chief of the confederate Canaanite forces). He consented to act on condition that Deborah would accompany him, for which reason he was told that not he, but a woman, would have the honor of despatching Sisera. The details of his victory, when a sudden downpour flooded the river Kishon and immobilized Sisera's chariots, are graphically depicted in the Song of Deborah, Judges 5:19–22—I think."[8]

"Don't you *know*?" I quipped.

"Hand me that Bible, please, Martha. Barak was written up in the faith chapter of Hebrews." Quickly he flipped the pages and found the spot.

" 'And what more shall I say? I do not have time to tell about Gideon, Barak, Samson, Jephthah, David, Samuel, and the prophets, who through faith conquered kingdoms, administered justice, and gained what was promised; who shut the mouths of lions, quenched the fury of the flames, and escaped the edge of the sword; whose weakness was turned to strength; and who became powerful in battle and routed foreign armies.' "[9]

"Wow!" I commented appreciatively. "Who was Jephthah?"

"I'm off duty now," he said, picking up his paper.

"Thanks, John." I kissed the top of his head—the thinning part. "I'll take a look outside for the guys. Should be bedtime soon."

On the way down the stairs I made a mental note to look up *Jephthah*.

Wrapping a coat around me against the early December evening air, I spied Mrs. O in her backyard.

"Yoo-hoo!" I waved enthusiastically. "Nice night, isn't it?"

She hefted a huge bag into her garbage can and walked over to the fence.

"Did you get the gingerbread boys?" I inquired cheerfully.

She wore a puzzled expression.

"I mean the cookies!" I smiled good-naturedly.

"Oh!" Her lips creased into a grin.

Just then Joe zoomed into our driveway on his bike. "Hi, Mom!"

"Say hello, Joe," I motioned my head in Mrs. O's direction.

"Hello!" He flashed a grin.

"See you later then!" I waved to my nebulous next-door neighbor and walked over to where Joe was standing next to his bike.

"Where's J.J.?" I watched as he pumped up his bike tires. "I thought he was with you."

"He was." Joe busied himself with his tires.

"So?" I put my hands on my hips in red-alert position.

"Take it eeeasy, Mom." He grabbed a wrench and began adjusting the seat. "This is too low. I'll get better power in my legs if I raise the seat."

"Joe." I commanded his attention. "John Junior."

"Oh, he's at Laura's."

Suspicion shot through my system like radio waves. In my mind's eye I saw my son walking hand-in-hand down the street with the blond-headed mermaid, and I muttered, "Minus her fins and flippers, of course."

"Say something, Mom?" Joe stood inside the door.

"Put away your bike, Joe."

"I just did!"

"Then get ready for bed."

"Mom, this is Joe you're talking to. I am not George. He goes to bed first." He crossed his arms on his chest. "He goes to bed first, and he's supposed to be asleep when I go to bed, but he never is. He always sits up and talks to me."

"Well, if you and J.J. hadn't fought all the time, you wouldn't have to share a room with George."

"Mom," he stated, leaning on the doorjamb, "I like sharing the room with George. At least he talks. J.J. was always writing letters to Babs . . ."

"Isn't he now?" I interrupted.

"Not as much, I guess." He looked at his shoes.

"Do you—"

"I'm sworn to secrecy!" He held up his hands. "Don't shoot!"

John Junior managed to slip in the house and into his room while I was fixing my hair for work the next day.

"Hi, J.J." I spoke from his bedroom doorway. "How was your bike ride?"

"Fine, Mom. I stopped by Laura's house."

"I know."

"Yeah, well, I've got a lot of homework to do, so I guess I better get at it." He smiled (in my opinion) guardedly. "Big bio test tomorrow!"

"Oh," I replied.

The next day, while checking groceries at Kleaver's, I mused about my offspring. "I gave them roots. Now I have to give them wings." I stuffed meat into a plastic bag. "John Jr. will be gone soon; probably married. After all, he graduates this year. It seems like last year he entered kindergarten." A tear filled my right eye, and I sniffed.

"That will be sixty-two dollars and fifty-five cents." I spoke to a nameless face across the counter.

During my lunchtime, I chewed my sandwich slowly. "I know J.J. is a person and all that now, but why a girl from the sea? Hasn't he read about the dangers of mermaids luring sailors to their deaths?" I crinkled up the plastic wrap and tossed it into the garbage. "It seems to me he should listen to me, instead of running over my opinions."

That evening, the perfection of Andrea Gray's melodious voice swept along the telephone lines and into my pain center. "Martha?" She waited for me to assimilate the information. "This is Andy."

"Oh, hi, I was thinking of calling you myself!" Bravely the mouse faced the lion.

"Oh, really?" She sounded interested.

"Yes, I was thinking we could study Deborah from the Book of Judges this year."

Silence.

"She's a good role model, and I was hoping to change our format from last year. I led the group, you know."

"Didn't the pastor tell you?"

My stomach sank out of sight. "Tell me?"

A lilting laugh lifted me out of my shoes before her statement gave me a right to the jaw. "I'll be leading the Women's Bible Study this year. You are too busy."

"Too busy?" My jaw went slack from the blow.

"Martha, we must have a bad connection. You keep repeating what I'm saying."

"Oh." I stood transfixed by betrayal.

"We'll be studying church terms this year, Martha. Most women are illiterate when it comes to terms."

My hackles raised. "Name a term, Andrea, and I'll give you a definition."

"Certainly," she replied evenly. "Try *clerestory*." She paused.

Not since spelling bees in school had my knees trembled and my stomach churned. "Clerestory?"

"How about *narthex*?" She went for the jugular.

The sands of life flowed out through my toes. "Oh."

"You see, Martha," she continued to tromp on my lack of knowledge, "most women aren't up on this sort of thing and it makes us appear—well—ignorant."

Unable to stand against her effervescent energy, I agreed to be at choir practice the following Thursday.

Choir rehearsal proved I was two feet tall weighing in at three hundred pounds. Dressed casually (the way I always was to sing after a hard day's work), I couldn't believe my eyes when Andrea appeared in a smart tweed suit with her customary low-heeled shoes.

"I'm going to be sick," I mentioned to the soprano next to me.

"And it is with great pleasure," the choir director began, "that I call upon Andrea Gray to be our lead soprano this year."

I slumped lower in my seat.

"She comes to us highly recommended. We are fortunate to have her talent, her energy, and her vast knowledge and experience available to our little choir."

Andrea Gray stood up and walked to the front.

"She should live in the front," I muttered to myself.

"What?" asked the alto on the other side of me.

Rubbing my eyes, I said, "I have a headache."

"Oh," she said, sitting back in her seat.

Andrea's voice will break the beams of the building, I thought while waiting for her to rev up her vocal chords.

"Lord, bless this church," she trilled.

"Excuse me," I commented to the soprano in the front row as I stumbled past her. "I think I'm going to be sick."

They never knew I'd left. From my station in the bathroom I could hear Andy's voice preparing to split the rafters and my heart into splinters.

Making my way back to rehearsal, I managed to finish out the evening. "Good night, everybody," I called out to the group.

"Good night, Martha," they chorused. "Get better soon!"

I'd reached the safety of the sanctuary door when Andy's voice rang above the others. "Martha?"

Hesitating, I calculated the distance to the door.

Using giant steps, Andrea covered the distance between me and her before I had time to shift my weight to my left foot. "Martha?"

"Oh, hello, Andrea. How are you?" I lied. I didn't care how she was and guilt flooded my soul.

"I wonder if you could wait a minute." Her raven black hair shone with quality grooming. "I am organizing a preschool choir, and I will need your preschoolers." Her snappy-black eyes melted my gaze.

"What will you need, Andrea?" My nerves strung themselves into a tight knot.

"It's perfectly simple, Martha. Since you're handling snack time as well, you can combine handing out cookies with making name tags for the children and getting them into line on Sunday mornings." She paused and waited for me to reply in the affirmative. "You *are* getting the cookies, aren't you?"

"I don't know—I—"

"Nonsense, Martha." She straightened her white collar. It blazed bright against her brown nubby tweed suit.

"Andrea," I began bravely, "I've never met your husband."

Her dark eyes bore into mine. Her stone expression remained placid. "No, you haven't."

"What does he do?" I dropped my gaze and twisted my fingers briefly. "I mean, for a living, of course." My left leg ached. I shifted my weight to my right foot. "I didn't mean to pry." My insides felt like jelly.

"Of course." Her thin nose twitched slightly. "He is a denturist."

"Of course!" I replied eagerly, not knowing a dentist from a denturist. "I'll have to come in and see him sometime."

"Martha, I am truly sorry. I didn't know you have dentures. The work is so well done it almost looks real!" Her look of amazement shocked me into a shameful speech.

"Actually few people know. I had it done by the best in the business. See you, Andrea!"

Driving home, I worried all the way. "Now she thinks I've got false teeth! Why didn't I just admit I didn't know what a denturist was? What if she tells John? Then he will know I lied. Oh, this is so embarrassing!"

I ran a stop sign and checked for flashing red lights. *By the time I get home I could be a criminal!*

Discomfort plagued me the rest of the evening, and I retired early with a headache.

The next morning at breakfast John said, "Pass the sugar, please, Martha. Are you feeling all right?"

"Why?" A cornered feeling swept up my spine.

"You've been having a lot of headaches lately."

"Maybe I should have my eyes checked too," I retorted.

At work my feet moved along like lead weights, and I retreated to the supply room to eat lunch. "I *need* to study Deborah. She must have known a few things I don't know, or other people wouldn't have asked her for advice. Maybe Andrea is like Deborah. Everybody seems to look up to her—even John." Fatigue felled me. I rested my head against my hands for a moment.

"Mrs. Christian!" The voice of Jimmy, the stock boy, forced me to my feet. "You're sleeping!"

Raising myself to my full height of five feet, I tried to look lean and mean. "Not sleeping, Jimmy—*meditating*. Something you would know nothing of." I folded my arms and waited.

Jimmy slapped his right thigh and laughed out loud. "You could have fooled me, Mrs. Christian. When I was *meditating*, *you* said I was sleeping!" He curled his fuzzy upper lip in disdain.

"Jimmy," I clipped my speech, "you are fired."

Whipping off his stock-boy apron, he threw it on the floor. "So who needs your crummy job!" He slammed out of the stock-room.

Angry tears stung, and my knees shook. "What have I done?"

It couldn't be undone. Jimmy had cleaned out his small locker before I could fix my face and return to work.

"Why did Jimmy quit, Mrs. Christian?" Ginny's nasal twang grated my nervous system.

"I fired him for sleeping," I responded mechanically. "Now let's count the cash and close the market."

During dinner, Jimmy's leaving haunted me.

After completing supper cleanup, I phoned him at home. "Hello, Jimmy?"

"Hullo, Mrs. Christian." He recognized my voice right away.

"About today . . ."

"I'm not coming back, Mrs. Christian. You yelled at me."

"Yes, I know. That's why I called." I smiled into the plastic receiver.

"I already called Mrs. Kleaver."

"Mrs. Kleaver?" Terror jolted my spine.

"She was very nice to me."

"I am certain she was, Jimmy." My mind flew at warp speed, wandering in areas surrounded by fear and uncertainty.

"So don't waste your time trying to talk me into coming back because I won't be back—ever." His monotone delivered its final summation.

"Oh," I responded before he cut the connection.

That night I dreamed I tried to manage Kleaver's on my own. The day after that my mother called from the coast. "Martha?"

"Mom! It's so good to hear from you! I can't wait until you visit for Christmas! Are you coming by plane, or train?"

"That's why I called, Martha. I won't be able to make it this year."

"Not make it?"

"Didn't you hear me, Martha?"

"Oh yes, Mom! For some unknown reason I've been repeating myself lately. That is, other people's statements."

"That's because you're upset about something, Martha. You did that as a child—usually on the first day of school, or just before an important exam. Sometimes you would repeat everything said, if you were under a great deal of stress . . ."

"That's okay, Mom. Really." I gathered a big breath, shoved down my disappointment, and inquired, "Are you all right?"

"Just fine, dear. Don't worry, but I had a small fall and broke my leg. The trip would be too hard for me, I'm afraid."

"Oh, Mom. I am so sorry. Certainly it would be too much.

"Once Mr. Kleaver has recovered from his heart attack, I'll come out to visit you." Trying to imagine my five-foot-tall, gray-headed mother in a leg cast, I asked, "Does it hurt?"

"I'm more concerned about your repeating phrases. Everything all right with you?"

"Yes!" I lied emphatically. "On another subject—remember how you used to tell stories about women in the Bible when I was little?"

A chuckle reassured me of her spiritual strength. "Who are you comparing yourself to this time, Martha?"

"Not comparing, Mom. More like exploring." Since she said nothing in reply, I plunged right ahead. "Deborah."

"She was a woman of calm wisdom, Martha . . ."

"Uh huh," I responded with confidence born of desperation. "How did she . . ."

My ever patient mother waited for me to continue. I realized, however, I didn't know what to ask next. "Thanks, Mom. Take care of yourself. We will miss you."

"I will be praying, Martha," she responded, as she always did.

Deeply troubled, I shoved through the next week with my hands busy, but my spirit in pain. "Lord, will I ever achieve tranquility under pressure?"

As Christmas approached, time disappeared in bunches. Somehow I acquired plain, cheap vanilla cookies for Sunday school snack time, herded my preschoolers into appropriate positions, explained to Mr. Kleaver about my firing Jimmy, moved through meals, dirty laundry, and shopping.

When Christmas Eve arrived, my present was delivered personally—the flu riddled my body with pain from head to foot.

While John Jr. squired Laura to the candlelight Christmas Eve service, I staggered around the house trying to cook a turkey. When John informed me he and Joe would be helping Andrea with chairs for the Christmas Concert, I couldn't argue because my head pounded with pain.

When Joe, however, called me a "nag bag" based on his "youth lessons on Proverbs 19:13," I lifted my voice into hoarseness before it vanished like the fleeting sun at day's end.

Christmas Eve, while John, John Jr., Laura, Joe, and George were at church enjoying the fruits of Andrea Gray's labor, I lay alone in my bed with tears trickling down my cheeks.

Specimen the dog, Buddy the bird, and Ben the senior-citizen guinea pig seemed to fill the empty house with love.

"Is this how it was with you, Lord?" I sniffed and blew my nose. "Lying in the manger, did you feel that the sheep, cows, and goats loved you more than people?"

Christmas, New Year's, and my stint of flu and self-pity passed. With the decorations packed away, the tinsel and pine needles vacuumed, the bright winter sunshine lifted my mood. "I am *well*!" I cheered myself along while enjoying a winter walk. Kicking up a small pile of snow, I watched the white whirl up before it settled back to the ground. "Mom said Deborah had wisdom. That can't be an impossibility."

Lifting my eyes to the blue sky, I inhaled deeply and decisively. "I will now speak wisdom. As I understand myself, I will become wise."

Turning around, I crossed the street and briskly shuffled my feet toward home. "I won't worry that Andrea Gray refuses to study Deborah this year. I will read about her, and I will learn, and I will speak wise words, and all this silly worry will pass."

Just then I passed Mrs. O's house. "I never noticed that before," I said to myself, slowing my pace. "What is that smokestack for?"

Turning into our driveway, I walked along the fence to the backyard and peered over it.

"Oh!" A shriek of fright greeted me.

"Hi there!" I waved my red mitten at her.

Holding a piece of some type of machinery, Mrs. O looked back at me blankly.

After a few failed attempts to communicate, I returned to my house to ponder the small structure which now sported a smokestack.

Later that evening, I tried to discuss the matter with John. "John, have you seen what the neighbors are building?"

With his back to me he replied, "Not now, Martha, I am really busy. I've been assigned to teach physical education for grade ten boys."

"That's nice," I responded calmly. "Now, about that smokestack. What do you think they're building?"

When he turned to look at me, his blue eyes cut like cold metal.

"You wouldn't treat Andrea Gray like this!" The words shot out of my mouth before I could catch them. Chagrined, I lamely added, "I guess P.E. isn't your first choice."

Immediately retreating to the winter climate of our backyard, depression slammed down and squished my soul. "The first bright day I've spent in weeks, and now I've started a quarrel with John." Pacing back and forth, the moonlight granted peace to the trembling trees.

Visions of Andrea Gray organizing my Sunday school class, monopolizing my husband, and ordering me to plunder cookies from Kleaver's Meats and Merchandise flashed a red-alert in my brain.

Squaring my shoulders, I faced the bitter cold. "Napoleon

rose from 1769 to 1821; therefore, I can rise to face Andrea Gray."

Shivering slightly, I adjusted my toque and looked toward the future.

Waterloo.

4 / Clambake

"Praise the Lord! Israel's leaders bravely led; the people gladly followed! Yes, bless the Lord!"[10]

"Want to go for a walk with me?" John asked, giving me a quick hug.

"Not now, John, I've got laundry to fold."

His look of disappointment escaped my attention as I pawed through the clean pile of clothes on the laundry table.

"Why aren't there any *socks* for George?" I muttered.

"I'm going then," he called as he opened the basement door.

"Bye," I responded, busily folding.

Barely aware of his leaving, I hollered upstairs, "George?" I drummed my fingers on the table top. "George!"

Nothing.

Stamping over to the foot of the stairs, I groused to myself, "I've got too much to do anyway. Why should I have to fold laundry at night? I don't see anyone else around this place down in the depths of the house. In the evening I should be sitting down enjoying myself, or reading a good book, or . . ." I waited for George to answer.

"George!" I screeched.

"Mom, what is your problem? I am trying to study." *Joe's* head appeared at the top of the stairs—where my youngest son's head should have been.

"Joe, please go get your brother," I said.

"Why?"

"What is this—this inquisition? Obviously the matter in question is between George and me."

"You yelled for J.J.—not George!"

"I did not! Open your ears! *J.J.* doesn't sound like *George!*"

"Sarcasm never works, Mom. It is beneath us. I'm learning that in school." He smiled slightly. "Let's just simmer down, shall we? I know you don't want to be like other parents who hate their kids just because they are teenagers." Resting his case, he folded his arms confidently.

My eyes sparked fire. Fury rose in my veins. I counted to ten. "Get *George*, Joe, before I get *you!*"

"Why would you say J.J. when you meant George?" His haughtiness threw me off guard for a moment.

Flames threatened to shoot from my mouth. I took two steps upward toward him.

"Are you feeling upset, Mom?" His proud look melted.

"George!" I screamed, ignoring my middle son.

"What!" The distant reply rang out.

"Get downstairs—now!" Turning on my heel, I marched back to the clean laundry waiting to be folded.

With great energy I creased shirts and tops, and other people's socks.

Almost immediately my youngest blue-eyed twelve-year-old appeared at my side. "Hi, Mom. Didja Call me?"

"Where are your *socks*, George?" I put my hands on my hips. "And, why didn't you answer when I called you?"

"I did, Mom," he replied, shoving his glasses higher on his nose with his forefinger. His braces glinted under the light of a bare bulb in the basement ceiling.

"Where is J.J.?" I queried, changing the subject.

"John Jr.?" He looked surprised.

"Yes, your brother who doesn't seem to live here anymore."

"Hmm," he said, stuffing his hands into his rumpled jean pockets, "that's a good question."

Smoothing sweaters with my hands, I remarked, "One child asks ridiculous questions; the other refuses to offer information."

"Now where are your socks?" A word foreign to his ears

seemed to glance off his consciousness.

As patiently as possible for a mother of three who had a full working schedule, a house to run, bills to pay, and a husband to love, I waited for him to reply.

Expecting a blank expression, I was unnerved by his worried countenance. He adjusted his rumpled shirt and twirled his light brown hair just like he used to do when he was a baby.

"Socks?" he said weakly.

"Oh no, George." I watched his face go crimson. "You didn't use them for *Ben*?"

"For padding, Mom. He needed it for his spaceship." His slight build seemed smaller than usual.

"How many pairs did you use?" I probed gently for information.

He shifted from his right foot to his left.

"All of them?" I didn't want to know.

Reading my face at incredible speed, and finding no intent of malice on my part, he broke into a shining smile. "I think I can find some foam or something."

"Good idea," I agreed good-naturedly. "I think I know where we have some."

By the time we'd located some stuffing for the guinea pig's spaceship, the laundry lay neatly in various drawers, my feet were propped up on a footstool, and my good humor had returned.

Just then I heard noises in the kitchen. "We already had dinner!" I shouted to whomever.

The fridge door opened, then closed.

"Is everyone hard of hearing around this house?" I muttered, listening more closely.

Cupboard doors opened and slammed shut.

"Who's out there now?" I yelled.

"Just me, Mom," Joe's adolescent bass responded.

"What are you doing?" Raising my voice seemed easier than moving my tired body to the scene of the action.

"Nothing, Mom," My brown-eyed, fifteen-year-old man-child replied. Meanwhile, the blender began to whir.

"Where is *John*?" I complained, hefting myself onto my feet.

"He should look after some of these things. I work all day, too."
Quick strides brought me to the kitchen.

"Hi, Mom!" Joe began buttering a piece of toast.

"Joe, we ate less than two hours ago. Why are you eating now?"

"Parents aren't supposed to ask 'why' questions, Mom. We learned that in school."

"And what's this?" I pointed to the pitcher of brown liquid.

"Eggnog, Mom. Chocolate. I need it for wrestling." He flexed a bicep and flashed a smile in my direction.

"Charming," I stated without enthusiasm. "Don't forget to clean up this mess."

"Sure, Mom," he answered, spilling the concoction on the counter.

Making my way back to the living room, I peered out our picture window. "My, that thing looks bigger than ever in Mrs. O's yard. Wonder what it is?"

Clucking affectionately to Buddy the bird on my way back to the sofa, I sat down, only to be interrupted by the jangling telephone just as I became comfortable.

"Somebody else can answer it," I muttered, picking up my knitting. "This blue scarf, for whomever, is two years overdue."

The telephone continued to irritate my nervous system.

"Somebody answer the phone!" I screamed, still trying to count stitches.

The constant jingle of the phone set my teeth on edge.

"Joe?"

No answer.

"Joe!" I yelled louder.

"Whaaat?" A distant almost-baritone responded.

"Never mind! I'll do it myself!" I shouted.

"*What*, Mom!" Joe's voice reverberated through the house.

"I said, *never mind!*" Hauling myself up on my feet, I hurried to pick up the receiver. The ringing stopped. "Terrific!" I turned around and headed back toward the sofa.

The phone rang again.

Racing back, I snatched the receiver before the telephone could clang three times. "Gotcha!"

Changing my tone to pure sweetness, I said into the receiver, "Hello?"

"Mom?" John Jr.'s voice called from the other end of the wire. "Where are you?"

"Laura's." The reply, so simple, devastated my insides. "I'm running behind time," he suggested smoothly.

"Get home, or I'll tell your father."

I hated myself all the way back to my knitting. "I should have been able to handle it better than that. J.J. should respect my wishes as much as John's."

I picked up the blue yarn just as the telephone rang again.

"Oh no," I moaned, slumping on the edge of my chair.

"I'll get it, Mom!" George careened down the hall toward the kitchen. "Gotta get a carrot for Ben anyway!"

I waited before I looped the yarn over my fingers.

"Hello?" George began. "Yeah? Oh, yeah! Sure, she can."

Leaping to my feet, panic rose as I realized I was the only *she* in the house. "George, who is it?"

Stuffing his finger into his free ear he continued. "No problem at all, Mrs. Gray."

"George, is that for me?" Frantically, helplessly, I gestured to my son who kept talking.

"Good idea, Mrs. Gray! Sure she can get carts from Kleaver's. I'll tell her right away!"

"George!" I leaped for the telephone and missed.

"Sure thing, Mrs. Gray!" He slammed down the receiver as I glared in futility.

"That was Mrs. Gray, Mom," he beamed in excitement. "She wants you to get some grocery carts. I told her you would." He smiled proudly.

"You *what*?" An explosive breath of air punctuated the *T*.

"Somethin' wrong, Mom?" He rummaged through the refrigerator.

"Yes, indeed, something is wrong, George!" I whipped around in front of him. "What did she *say*? And what are you doing?"

"Just what I said she said," George responded, his voice muffled in the refrigerator. "I have to get a carrot for Ben!"

"All right. Just a carrot." I stepped back. "George, why did you take my telephone call!"

His puzzled eyes pleaded for mercy before they filled with tears. He shook his head.

"Look, honey, I'm sorry. It's just that I can't get carts for Mrs. Gray." I put my right arm around his shoulders.

His face rekindled a flame of hope. "Sure you can, Mom! You can do anything you set your mind to do!" He wiped his eyes with his shirt-sleeve. "That's what you always tell me!"

"I'll call her myself, George. Thanks anyway."

"You bet, Mom!" And he disappeared.

Heavily I dragged my feet to the telephone. Hesitantly I pushed the buttons on the phone. Great discomfort washed over me as I listened to the ringing at the other end. One ring, two rings, three rings . . .

"Guess she's not home," I cheered.

"Andrea! Hello!" I guiltily warbled.

"Martha?" I winced as her voice pierced through the lines. "You picked a terrible time to call," she replied.

"Excuse me." I shrank into my shirt collar. "Did I interrupt something?"

Silence.

"Yes, well, I am sorry that I called at an inopportune time—"

"What is it, Martha?" she rudely inquired.

"Well, I'm returning your telephone call to find out about, uh, carts from Kleaver's." I took a deep breath, hating my cowardice in speaking to the nemesis of my self-esteem.

"Oh yes, Martha. I settled that with George." Her tone seemed rather superior.

Anger rose, threatening to explode on Mrs. Commander In Chief of the local church army. "Settled what?"

"You will supply three grocery carts." The announcement made, she waited.

"Might I ask what for?"

"Really, Martha, I don't have time for this, but I will explain it to you. You could have warned me if you were not going to cooperate."

Her insult sliced into my heart like a paring knife to butter.

"Well," I backed off immediately, "if you can't tell me now, maybe later." I rubbed my wrist across my forehead in embarrassment.

She expounded for nearly an hour about her newest program for our little church—"Carts for the Underprivileged Poor."

Andrea formulated the plan to meet our community's needs for relief during times of unemployment, acts of God (hurricanes, tornadoes, floods, and earthquakes, she explained), and sickness and health problems of catastrophic proportions.

"C.F.T.U.P.," she continued, "will promote God's cause in our world—first on a small-town basis, and then—who knows?" Her voice took on a dreamy quality.

"Why do you call it C.F.T.P.U.?" I inquired, duly subdued.

"CARTS FOR THE UNDERPRIVILEGED POOR— C.F.T.U.P., Martha," she corrected, as teacher to pupil. "Write it down. Then you will remember."

Dutifully, I doodled it on a scratch pad next to the telephone. "Looks like something off my eye doctor's wall," I joked.

"It's pronounced, 'Sef-tup,' Martha," she huffed.

Trying to compute "Sef-tup" in my mind, I came up with nothing and decided it was probably better not to pursue it at the moment.

"I can't get the carts," I stated flatly.

She sighed with perfect control. "Don't be silly, Martha. What are a couple of carts among friends?"

"I had trouble enough getting the cookies," I defended. "I'm paying for them out of my own earnings. I can't afford to buy a cart!"

"We'll need *three*," she replied, impervious to my suffering.

"I can't get *one*!" I begged.

"Nonsense, Martha," she answered smoothly. "*Can't* means *won't*."

That one stopped me. *Won't* seemed an ugly word, unworthy of my standing as a Christian wife and mother.

"Think about it, Martha. You will come up with a cart. I am certain of it."

A vision of maggots flashed before my eyes. I knew she remembered the worms in the candy from Kleaver's, but would she tell anyone at church? I shivered at the thought of tiny, white wiggling creatures taking up residence in chocolate. "Disgusting!" I blurted.

"What?" she threatened in return.

"Nothing," I quickly answered. "I was thinking out loud. I'll see what I can do," I resigned.

"Fine," she exulted. "And, Martha, there's another matter of importance to discuss . . ."

I held my breath.

"Your book. The one I borrowed a couple of Sundays ago? I'll put it outside my back door in a brown paper bag, with your name on it, and you can collect it tomorrow on your way home from work."

"Anything else?"

"Yes. Don't call me again at this time of evening. It is inconvenient for me. I take a small rest every evening after supper. I'd like you to respect that."

Dismissed, I cut the connection with disdain.

The next day, as ordered, I arrived after work at Andrea Gray's castle. The door was shut, her sleek car preened in the driveway, and a small brown bag lay beside the back door. Picking it up gingerly, I plodded to my car and drove home in defeat.

"To live is to bleed," I decided.

While everyone else was out after dinner, I opened my favorite ragged version of the Bible. "Praise the Lord! Israel's leaders bravely led; the people gladly followed! Yes, bless the Lord! Listen, O you kings and princes, for I shall sing about the Lord, the God if Israel. When you led us out from Seir, out across the fields of Edom, the earth trembled and the sky poured down its rain. Yes, even Mount Sinai quaked at the presence of the God of Israel! In the days of Shamgar and of Jael, the main roads were deserted. Travelers used the narrow, crooked side paths. Israel's population dwindled, until Deborah became a mother to Israel."[11]

"A mother to Israel!" My eyes looked back into time and forward to the future. I slapped the book shut and saw myself singing God's praises after leading my army to victory. The sight was pleasant to behold. *I am a mother*, I reasoned. *A very tired one, however.* I lay down on the sofa and slept.

"Martha?" John shook my shoulder slightly. "Feeling all right?"

"Hi, honey!" I said, bolting upright. "Back from your walk?"

"Pretty chilly out there," he remarked, rubbing his hands together.

"Guess I fell asleep." I stood up and straightened my sore back. "Got a question for you, John. What did Jephthah have in common with Deborah?"

John's blue eyes twinkled. "Jephthah who?"

"You know, John, Jephthah who judged Israel for six years,[12] and who delivered Israel from the oppression of the Ammonites."[13]

"I don't see the connection." He smoothed his thinning hair back over his head.

"The connection is," I explained like a hare to a tortoise— "Deborah also judged Israel, and she delivered the Israelites from the Canaanites."

"Uh huh." My husband furrowed his brow.

"She was a *woman!*" Triumphantly I waited for his understanding. "Yesterday I was reading about Jephthah, and he was a *man* . . ."

"I don't get it," he responded.

"I wonder how she did it? Nobody ever listens to me."

"Are you saying a woman can't do what God calls her to do?"

"What?" I wrinkled my eyebrows together.

"Let's get some rest, Martha. You look feverish."

By the next morning, I felt almost well enough to go to church.

George appeared beside my bed bearing a breakfast tray of tea and toast.

"Dad said to bring you this. We're having pancakes, and eggs, and sausages . . ."

"Who's cooking?" In my mind's eye I could see the kitchen dripping with pancake goo, sausages lying on the floor for Specimen, and eggs oozing down the kitchen drawers.

"Dad!" George beamed. "He says we men have to stick together when you're sick!"

Gratefully I sipped the tea and nibbled on the toast.

"Martha?" John poked his head into our bedroom. "How's the patient?"

"How sweet of you, John! I knew I married well, but you're the top!"

"We aim to please, my dear!" With a towel over his arm, and a Cheshire grin, he swept my tray away and covered me up to my nose. "Now sleep. That's orders from headquarters."

After they left, I crept out of the bed to read more about Jephthah and discovered the vow he made to God: "If you give the Ammonites into my hands, whatever comes out the door of my house to meet me when I return in triumph from the Ammonites will be the Lord's, and I will sacrifice it as a burnt offering."[14]

Reading on, I discovered the first person to come out of his house was his only daughter! "I guess the lesson here is not to make a vow to God unless I mean it!" Unable to determine whether or not Jephthah actually offered his only child, or whether she was doomed to a life of perpetual celibacy, I put my head on my pillow and slept.

The rest of the day passed in a haze of headache, upset stomach and fever.

Monday morning, I dragged myself to work.

Thursday evening, I felt too sick to attend the church clambake (arranged instead of choir practice in order to celebrate the opening of Andrea's latest contribution to our world—the new church library).

Meanwhile, I suffered at home. "I could fry a few clams on my feverish forehead," I murmured, rubbing my sore eyes.

John related the details. "Excellent cuisine, Martha. Sorry you missed it." He peered at himself in our bedroom mirror. "Andrea has appointed me to head up the library project, and I've accepted."

The next day I marched back to work at Kleaver's. "I can originate a few projects of my own!" I snarled as I created new displays, wrote bigger and better newspaper advertisements, and organized tempting meat exhibits. I buried my anger and jealousy among the steaks and roasts.

Stacking tomatoes, I remarked, "Andrea Gray's hold on my family, my church, and yes, the entire community squeezes me into nothingness. I am a nobody whom nobody listens to!"

My eldest son, John Jr., instead of helping around the house, spent his time with Laura, or his dog, Specimen. Communication between us ceased. Strife took over instead.

"J.J., get that dog *outside* where he belongs!"

"It's cold out there!" His blue eyes flashed anger.

"The dog has a fur coat!"

"It's February!" My son delivered a heavy blow.

"What?" I stood before him totally confused.

"People should treat animals with respect!" His jaw set, his face darkened with anger. "If that's the way it is around here, then I'm moving into the dog house with him!"

"You don't have to move in—you're already in the dog house!" Sore of spirit, weary of body, I said things I didn't mean.

John Jr. retreated deeper into himself.

"Why? Jean," I moaned to my dearest friend on the telephone.

"Because he's growing up. He needs to separate himself now as an individual, Martha," she comforted with her usual warmth.

"I never hear Andrea Gray complain about her children," I confessed guiltily.

"Didn't you know?" Jean's voice rose in surprise.

"Know what?" I repeated.

"Andy doesn't have any children," she confided.

"I didn't know . . ."

"Don't say I told you, but it's been a sore spot in her marriage for years."

"Would you say she is, uh, happily married?"

"Now, Martha, why would you ask a question like that?"

Shortly after that exchange we concluded our conversation, but for the first time in fifteen years, I felt estranged from Jean.

The flu dragged on until I developed a deep cough that wouldn't go away.

"Better get that checked," John advised.

"I will," I agreed.

"So what do you think it is?" I said to the tired-looking physician.

"I don't know," he replied, writing on his prescription pad, "but I want you to get a few tests."

Dutifully I dragged myself to the laboratory where they failed several times to find a suitable vein to fill the waiting vial.

Then I shuffled my sick body to the X-ray department to have pictures taken of my lungs.

Finally, I sat before a doctor who didn't appear much older than J.J. "Where's the other one?" I queried politely.

"Other one?" He raised his black, bushy eyebrows above his spectacles.

"Never mind," I responded quietly. "It's just that I usually see the other doctor." I folded my hands in my lap in embarrassment. "He knows me," I explained.

"Oh"—his eyebrows dropped back down—"I'm sorry. My name is Dr. Young." He read the reports on his desk, leaned back, and inquired, "Have you ever had a TB test?"

"Look, really." Impatiently I leaned forward in my chair. "Can't you just give me something to get rid of the cough? I'm working, and I have three children, and my husband . . ." Tears filled my eyes.

"There, there, Mrs. Christian. You aren't feeling well, are you?"

"That's why I'm here," I sniffed. "I'm sorry. I'm not upset, I—"

"You just go and get this little test done for me, won't you? Then we can make a diagnosis." He spoke to me as though I couldn't have shown him how to cross the street!

Without a fight, I yielded my arm to be poked with tuberculin solution.

After a couple of blurred days, I arrived for my moment of truth.

This time I didn't bother to ask where either of the other doctors were; I just waited with my head pressed against the wall, next to the chair I'd collapsed into.

"Good news, Mrs. Christian!" The white-coated stranger piped. "Bronchitis!"

"What about TB?" I questioned wearily.

"TB?" She looked confused.

"Never mind," I answered, accepting the prescription. "This is fine."

Once back home, I noticed the family no longer had any patience for my sickness. Gone were the little love notes from George, the tea and toast from John.

The housework piled up, the laundry multiplied in the baskets, and the refrigerator accumulated half-eaten food that should have been discarded.

"Joe, couldn't you have thrown out these mashed potatoes?" I complained at my middle son.

"Want to see my new wrestling hold?" he replied, grabbing my arm cheerily.

"Just get out of the kitchen if you're not going to help."

"Sorry, Mom," he mumbled on his way to wrestling practice.

"Me too," I responded, as I ran after him and gave him a hug.

Resolving that self-pity would not capture me in its ugly claws, I began walking in the early evening to build my strength and clear my cough.

"January has been a long month, Lord," I whispered as I walked along by myself.

"John and I seem to be drifting apart, Joe breaks my arm every time he walks past, John Jr. doesn't need me anymore, and George is—well—just George."

I walked a little faster when I heard a foreboding noise behind me in a dark section of the street.

"What did Deborah have that I don't have? She rose to the position of a judge of Israel; men came to her for help in their time of need, and—"

I froze at the footsteps matching mine about a half-block behind me.

"Lord, with your help, I can be an exciting wife. John won't want to spend so much time with Andrea—even if she does have beauty, intelligence, and wit. I can't blame him for enjoying her company. After all, I haven't been around much lately."

Rounding the corner toward our house, I quickened my stride. The footsteps behind me clicked faster on the rough sidewalk.

I'm almost home, I thought, fear rising in my chest. *I'll jog the rest of the way.*

Breaking into a run, I didn't look back. But the terror of the nameless being that followed me paled in comparison to what stood in our driveway: Andrea's car.

5 / Fred

"Village life in Israel ceased, until I, Deborah, arose a mother in Israel."[15]

Settling myself in the dentist-like cold black chair, I lifted my chin as a large vinyl apron was fastened around my neck. "Feeling creative today?" I smiled brightly to the young hairdresser.

She pulled my hair knowingly out at the sides. "Getting a thin spot on top of your head," she announced matter-of-factly.

"Really?" Shards of panic shot up my neck and I shivered.

"Sit still, please," she instructed.

"Sorry, I haven't been well."

Chewing her gum vigorously, coupled with her nasal twang, roasted my personhood. "Well, when ya get, ya know . . . older . . . ya get those times." She tightened the noose around my neck and roughly grabbed a lock of my hair with her right hand, while poising her scissors with her left.

"Are you left-handed?" I inquired uneasily.

"Naw," she replied, flipping the shears into her right hand with a surgical snap, "my right hand is sore today."

Unable to believe she would cut a hair of my head with the wrong hand, I asked, "What's wrong with it?"

Scrunching up her face, she thought for a moment. "I twisted my wrist playing ball, I think." She shoved my head into cutting position. "It's okay. I'll go ahead anyway."

My frayed nervous system caused me to flinch as she grabbed a piece of hair next to my ear.

"Jumpy, aren't ya," she commented, whizzing the first cut up the side of my head.

Like George's guinea pig, Ben, who froze into a statue at the slightest alarm, I stiffened.

"You got nothin' to worry about, though," she continued, whacking away around my ear. "I'm good, and I'm fast."

The fruity smell of her gum overpowered the odors of hair spray and other potions sitting on the counter nearby.

"Yessir," she said as she snipped, "I'm not like some hairdressers. Why, I heard of one who even cut a patron's ear . . ."

Just then I felt the pain in my left ear lobe.

"Hmm," she stated, grabbing a cloth, "your hair grows too close to your ear on this side."

Unable to speak from the shock of imagining blood running from my nicked ear, I squirmed uncomfortably.

"Sit still," she complained. As she whipped my chair away from the mirror I could only guess what was coming.

"These scissors are no good," she muttered, while cutting away. "You sure came on a bad day."

Trying to be patient, I replied, "Well, I guess we all have our days."

"There!" she announced, whirling me around to face my image.

Words could not explain how I felt when I saw my head. "I can see my head," I whimpered.

"You said you wanted me to *cut it*, didn't you?" She sounded angry.

"Yes, of course, I wanted it cut, but—"

"Look here, everybody! Isn't this a great style?" She waved her arms and pointed at my shorn scalp.

Somehow I shuffled my way out of the shop and into the cold February air. "Frostbite," I whispered to myself. "I'm going to have frostbite. Then I'll catch a cold . . ." Just then I saw Andrea Gray walking down the street toward me.

Quick! Hide! my brain exclaimed as I rushed into a clothing store.

Grabbing a hat off a display, I shoved it on my head.

"May I *help* you?" A female voice approached me from behind.

"Just looking," I replied, ripping the chapeau from my skull.

"Oh my"—her sympathetic tone disturbed me—"have you been ill?"

"What?" I glanced out the store window and spied Andrea looking in.

"I mean, my dear, your hair." She stared thoughtfully at my scalp. "Have you been having *treatments*?"

"Treatments?" My eyes widened in horror as I saw Andrea move toward the front door. "Yes! I need a hat!"

Snatching a fox fur hat, I pulled it down over my ears and announced, "I need a fitting room!"

Peeking out from the curtain, I watched Andrea Gray swirl around the room. Finally she left.

The gray-haired clerk comforted me as I tried on an assortment of head coverings. "Don't worry, dear, lots of people have treatments and lose their hair. At least you're still alive!"

"I might as well be dead," I moaned, moving on to wigs.

By the time I arrived home, I felt like I'd been to boot camp instead of a beauty salon.

Fortunately, no one saw me creep into the house and race up the stairs to the bathroom mirror.

"Oh, oh, oh!" I gasped unintelligibly.

By the time dinner was over, my self-confidence vanished.

"It's okay, Mom," counseled George. "Buddy doesn't look too good when he's molting either."

"Never mind," I responded in pain.

"Yeah," chimed Joe, "first you'll get all picky looking, and then you'll have hair!" He reeled off to his room laughing all the way.

"You should have joined a religious order," said John Jr.

"That's enough, kids," interjected John. "Now go do your homework."

"Thanks," I replied.

"It'll grow," he responded, helping to clear the table. "I love you"—he gave me a kiss on my head—"new haircut and all."

He managed to dodge the wadded up napkin I threw at him.

The next morning, I faced my dilemma. "According to Madame de Stael, to know all is to forgive all," I decided, combing my fuzzy scalp with a baby comb. "I will forgive the hairdresser."

By the time I arrived at work and took my place at Mr. Kleaver's desk, I dared anyone to mention my hair by giving a steely glance to whoever passed by the door.

I telephoned my boss's residence. "Mrs. Kleaver?"

"Yes, Martha!" Her friendly voice always reminded me of Mrs. Santa Claus.

"I was wondering if, or *when*, Mr. Kleaver will be able to come back to work."

"Is anything wrong?" Concern clouded her cheerfulness.

"Does anything have to be wrong?" I chuckled a little to give her confidence.

"Oh no, dear. It's just that you sound a little upset."

"Nonsense!" I lied without a trace of guilt. "My hair should grow back by spring," I said to myself under my breath.

"You just wanted to give us a ring? How nice!"

"Actually, I need to hire someone to replace Jimmy, the stock boy who kept sleeping on the job. Can you ask Mr. Kleaver about that?"

"Certainly, Martha. Wait just a moment."

While holding the receiver with my chin and left shoulder, by habit I ran my hand over my head and felt picks instead of locks. Closing my eyes in agony, I felt thankful I'd escaped running into Andrea. *It will only be a matter of time*, I thought, misery creeping up my spine.

"Martha?" Mrs. Kleaver's voice broke into my reverie. "Mr. Kleaver says that's fine. Hire another stock boy. Is there anything else?"

"No," I replied dismally. "I'll put an advertisement in the paper right away."

"Will that be all then, dear?"

"No!" Taking the bull by the horns, I explained Andrea's need for carts, concluding with, "I can understand perfectly that this is probably a preposterous request."

"Just a minute, dear."

Left holding the telephone, I wondered where I could have come up with the courage to ask.

"That's fine, Martha," Mrs. Kleaver stated simply.

"Fine?" The telephone quivered in my nervous grip.

"Yes, Martha," she responded brightly. "He says that any friend of yours is a friend of his."

"But she wants *three*! Won't you be short?"

"He says that it's fine, Martha."

Realizing no more discussion was necessary, I let the matter rest, and said goodbye.

"Not only does *Andy* run the church, and my family, now she runs the store!" Still grumbling to myself, I pulled out a piece of paper and a felt-tipped pen to draft an ad for a new stock boy.

"WANTED! BOY FOR STOCK WORK WHO WON'T SLEEP ON THE JOB!" I began directly.

Looking over my work, I decided, *Maybe that sounds too negative.* Leaning back in my chair and rubbing my eyes, I assumed a better posture, and scratched out "FOR STOCK WORK."

"Mrs. Christian?" My name, punctuated by the loud sound of cracking gum, unnerved me. Ginny, my best cashier, appeared.

"Yes, Ginny," I replied, keeping my eyes glued to the paper before me.

"A lady was here, saying she'd come for three grocery carts. I told her she couldn't have them, but she wheeled them right out of the store!"

"Maybe I better leave 'FOR STOCK WORK' in after all," I responded without hearing anything but the snapping gum.

Ginny began to wave her arms. "Mrs. Christian! Somebody stole *three carts*!" Her frizzed bleached-blond hair stood out in every direction from her scalp.

"Calm down, Ginny," I soothed; "nobody . . ." Visions of Andrea Gray gave me goose bumps. "Was she tall?"

"Yes!" My best checker squeaked in alarm.

"Did she have jet-black hair?"

"Yes!" Ginny's eyes rolled in their sockets. "How did you know?"

"I know these things," I calmly replied. "Don't worry about

it. Mr. Kleaver says it's all right."

"Oh," she sighed, leaning back against the wall. "Well, I wish somebody would have told me."

"Why?" I inquired, half-interested.

"Because I called the police!"

Instantly alert, I jumped out of my chair and grabbed Ginny by the shoulders. My mouth opened and shut itself while words refused to form themselves on my lips.

Ginny burst into sobs. "Oh no, oh no, oh . . ."

"Police?" I whispered the word. "You called the blue-coats?" Goose bumps formed on my knees. I couldn't imagine Andrea Gray in handcuffs. I could, however, imagine me tarred, feathered, and carried out of town on a rail when the good folks at church found out I'd been responsible for arresting their crusader, their saint of the poor and impoverished, their—

"Mrs. Christian!" Ginny's voice broke through. It was her turn to shake my shoulders.

Blankly, I turned my vacant gaze in her direction.

"It's over!"

"Over?" I repeated the word slowly. "Yes, it's all over now."

"I mean," she said, dragging me back to my chair, "it's fine now."

Slumping into my seat, I waited to hear the worst.

"Once the lady called the police *chief*, there was no problem."

"I'm going to be sick," I responded.

"Oh, Mrs. Christian!" she squealed and wrung her hands. "I can't stand it if anything happens to you after Mr. Kleaver already dropped over!" Pulling her gum out of her mouth, she stretched it out from her teeth with her thumb and forefinger.

"Stop sniveling!" Straightening my spine, I addressed the situation. "Start from the beginning, please."

By the time Ginny arrived at the end of her story, I knew I was standing in water over my head, bubbling at about 212 degrees Fahrenheit. "Well, it's too late to do anything about it now, Ginny. I'll think about it later."

"There's one other thing, Mrs. Christian," my gum-snapping employee announced on her way out the door; "there's someone here who says he wants to hire on as a stock boy." Ginny cracked her gum afresh.

"Really?" I rubbed my nose with my wrist. "That was fast."

"Fast?" Ginny paused and looked puzzled.

"I just drafted the advertisement for the newspaper, and here he is!" I clapped my hands excitedly.

Her blank expression informed me of the vacancy of our communication. Pulling a fresh stick of gum from her uniform pocket, she shoved it into her mouth.

"Tell him to come in, please." I waved her out the door while busily clearing away papers.

Within moments, a boy of average height appeared before my desk. His lank brown hair gave him a bedraggled appearance.

The telephone rang. Motioning for him to sit down, I picked up the receiver. "Kleaver's Meats and Merchandise," I intoned cheerily.

"Martha?" The voice shot panic to my pain center.

"Why, hello, Andrea! I was just going to call you," I lied.

"After all I've done for you, Martha, I would have expected a better reception."

"Reception?"

"You know exactly what I mean, Martha. Not only did you not have the three carts delivered as I expected, I was nearly arrested for stealing!" Her tone should have melted the receiver in my hand.

Guilt swept over me. My fingers began to twitch.

"Now," she continued, "I'll overlook it this time—especially because I talked to Mr. Kleaver."

Anger shunted guilt aside, until fear monopolized my emotions. "You talked to Mr. Kleaver?"

"Yes," she replied, cat-to-mouse. "*He* was most cooperative. He said you have been extremely busy and it was probably an oversight."

Feeling helpless, I said nothing.

"And then of course, I reminded him of other store managers who would be glad to contribute to *Sef-tup*."

"Other store managers?"

"I really haven't any more time to waste on this conversation, Martha—especially if you are just going to repeat what I am saying."

Beads of perspiration formed along my hairline as she terminated our one-way conversation.

Gently I placed the receiver on the telephone and tried to turn my attention to the young man sitting on the other side of my desk. "Hello!, uh . . ."

"Uh . . . Fred!" His hazel eyes turned soulfully in my direction.

"Yes, Fred." I nodded my head in affirmation. "Hello, Fred." Realizing I'd never hired anyone in my life, I didn't know what to do next. "So!" Smiling brightly, I picked up a pencil and piece of paper. "I should take a few notes."

"It's okay." He flipped his long, lank hair out of his eyes. "You don't have to hire me." Sniffling, he rose out of his chair.

"Are you sick?"

"Just a little cold," he snuffled, rubbing his nose with his sleeve. "I couldn't sleep last night."

"Couldn't sleep?" Instantly my mothering instincts took over. "Let me feel your head." Placing my wrist on his steaming forehead, I announced. "Hot!"

"It's nothin'," he responded, pulling back.

"It is too!" I shot back, shoving him back into his chair. "Now, you can't be more than twenty years old—"

"Nineteen," he interjected.

"Nineteen," I agreed. "Now, where is your mother? How can she let you job hunt in this condition?"

Slumping into his seat, he replied softly, "I don't have a mother."

"No *mother*?" My eyebrows rose in horror as my mind drifted back to something I'd recently read about Deborah—"Village life in Israel ceased, ceased until I, Deborah, arose, arose a mother in Israel."[16]

His shoulders hunched, he hung his head.

Bells pealed, trumpets sounded, and bass drums boomed in my brain. "A clarion call to action!" Instantly alert, my computer mind whirred into motion. So what if Andrea took over the rest of the world? I had my calling too! What could be better than taking care of a poor unfortunate boy who had no mother? Would my own children miss their mother these days? Why, they didn't even know when I was gone—unless, of course, it interfered with their stomachs . . .

Leaning forward over my desk, I asked gently, "Fred, you would never sleep on the job, would you?"

He lifted his feverish face. "No, Ma." His cheeks flushed red next to the dark shadows under his eyes. "I mean, ma'am."

My maternal tendencies responded as surely as dawn to the rising sun. "You may call me Ma if you like. Where do you live, Fred?"

"In a garage." Fred's shoulders rounded themselves as he stirred himself to speak.

"*Garage*?" I almost shouted. "What does your father do? Where is he? Why would he let you live in a garage? Didn't you bring the car home on time?"

Tugging at the neck of his tattered T-shirt, he replied, "I don't have a father either."

"Oh my! You poor dear!" In a flash I sealed our fate. "You're hired, Fred. Now take two days off while I think this over. We can't have you living in a garage . . ."

" . . . with no heat," he interjected.

"No heat!" Quickly I grabbed a blanket kept in my office for emergencies and handed it to him. "Take this and go home and try to get some rest."

Slowly he stood to leave. "Thanks, ma'am."

"You are very welcome, dear." I looked at his sallow skin. "Have you seen a doctor?"

"No—"

"—medical insurance. I understand. Take a couple of cans of chicken noodle soup on your way out and tell Ginny to charge them to the store. Call if you need me."

After Fred limped out of my office, I telephoned Mr. Kleaver to inform him of my managerial decision. Once Mrs. Kleaver brought him the telephone, I explained, "Mr. Kleaver, I've hired a young man named Fred. I am certain he will be fine."

"Why did you do that?" My employer's voice sounded weak.

"I thought Mrs. Kleaver told me you said it would be all right for me to hire another stock boy. Besides, Mr. Kleaver, Fred doesn't have any parents, he lives in a garage, and he is sick."

"I remember now, Martha—to replace Jimmy. That's all right."

Since he didn't mention Andrea Gray's three carts, or her subsequent conversation with him, neither did I.

The rest of the day flew by in a frenzy of activity. Not since my first dawn of motherhood had I felt so necessary.

That evening I approached John boldly. "John, I need a microwave oven!"

His blue eyes carefully considered me.

"Andy Gray has one. Jean told me. I have too much work and too little time to do it." I rested my nonassertive case.

John stared at me with his now-what-are-you-up-to look.

I wrinkled my nose in concentration. "Well? Aren't you going to say anything?"

"Do I have a choice?" he inquired.

"Not really," I replied with a smirk. "Mr. Kleaver sells them at the store, so I've already picked out a good one and had it charged against my paychecks."

His eyebrows drew in as his blue eyes clouded. "Oh," he replied distantly.

"Thank you," I said saucily and departed.

The next day I hurried home with my new prize. That evening I served rubber turkey—two hours late.

The following morning at Kleaver's, however, I scurried around like a mouse in a new house building a nest for her young.

By the following week, Fred's flu had flown the coop.

"Fred, get these ugly boxes out of the staff room, will you?"

"Sure, Ma!"

Pushing old straight chairs and step stools out of the way, I held up the new royal purple fabric I'd chosen to dress the windows in the staff room. "What do you think, Fred?"

"Looks great!" His freshly cut hair gleamed bright and clean under the bare bulb in the staff room. I wondered where he had received his haircut. "Where do you want them?"

"The stockroom would be nice, thank you." Placing the drapery material on a nearby table, I asked Fred, "Did you ever find another place to live?"

"Nope, but I'm workin' on it!" Fred began stacking boxes. "There's a basement apartment I could get right now if—"

"—if you had the money?"

"Yeah, sort of." Fred hung his head for a moment.

"Consider it done, Fred, my boy!" I whipped my checkbook out of my purse and poised my pen. "How much?"

"Oh, I couldn't accept that, Mrs. Christian," Fred stated firmly.

"How *much*, Fred?" My voice took on a managerial quality. "I can't.

"Consider it a loan until your first payday. Now, how much?"

"Two hundred and fifty dollars."

Quickly I wrote the check, tore it from the book, and handed it to him. "From your ma," I said gently, pressing the signed check into his hand. "Now get to work!"

"Yes, ma'am—uh—Ma!" Faster than a speeding snowplow, he cleared the room of boxes and trash.

Three days later, I'd curtained the staff room windows in purple. Ginny and Fred stood admiring my handiwork.

"Looks terrific, Ma!" Fred commented enthusiastically.

"Sure does, Ma!" chimed Ginny.

Ginny's new title for me didn't go unnoticed. Giving each of my employees a quick hug, I suggested, "Let's construct a Sharing Box for employee concerns, ideas, and troubles of a personal nature."

"Great! I'll get going on it right away," offered my adopted son.

"Good!" Ginny agreed. "I'll get the suggestion pad ready." She clapped her hands together excitedly. "Where shall we put it?"

"How about just outside my office door?" I beamed like the morning sun. "What shall we call it?"

"Call what?" Ginny looked confused.

"Everything has to have a name, Ginny," I advised knowingly.

"How about 'Employee's Suggestion Box?' " Fred plunged right in.

"By the way, Fred, did you get moved in?"

"Sure did, Ma!"

"Moved in?" Ginny turned confused eyes toward Fred.

"She's the *greatest*, Ginny!" Fred's hazel eyes twinkled, his shoulders squared, and his chest grew a couple of inches. "Ma Christian advanced me enough money to move out of that leaky garage and into a warm, dry basement." He patted my graying, drab-brown (and still short) hair.

"Nonsense, Fred," I blushed mildly. "It was nothing."

"We could call it a 'Sharing Box,' " suggested Ginny.

Smoothing my eyebrows with my fingers, I pondered a moment. "I have it!" Quickly I grabbed a piece of paper and wrote, "BOX FOR THE UNSUNG EMPLOYEE—B.F.T.U.E." I held it up for them to see.

"Isn't it kind of long?" Fred titled his head.

"We could call it BFTUE (pronounced Bif-too) for short!"

Ginny began to jump up and down. "Just perfect for Kleaver's Meats!"

"Meats?" It was my turn at confusion.

"Beef!" She chuckled in delight.

In only a week's time, all the employees had dropped ideas in the B.F.T.U.E., and I moved on to other things.

Gathering my staff together for a special lunch, I announced, "From now on, we will have a Power Hour for lunch break. That means you can eat for a half-hour—and rest, shop, do crafts, or whatever for the other half-hour!"

"Hooray!" they cheered.

"Good! I'm glad you're pleased!" Basking in the warmth of their praise, I threw myself into my self-designed tasks.

A few days later, I managed to change all the tattered red price tags to shiny new yellow ones. "Delivering Mr. Kleaver's staff from the bondage of clutter and rag-tag attempts at pricing items isn't exactly delivering the Israelites, but then Deborah didn't work in a supermarket either," I assured myself while washing the front windows.

By the end of February I'd developed a directory for my employees. "Mr. Kleaver will be so pleased when he returns!" I crooned happily. "Now each employee's birthday, anniversary, and other special dates will be recorded and duly celebrated."

The highlight of my work culminated in a winter picnic—complete with hot chocolate and marshmallows, honoring Fred for his steady service as our newest employee.

While my staff huddled around the fire, I sat under a frozen tree, admiring my work. "I may not be the mother of Israel," I chuckled to myself, "but I am godmother to my staff's children, and Ma Christian to everyone who shops in our store." Gazing over at the happy group, I sighed with satisfaction.

Ma.

6 / Stars

"From the heavens the stars fought, from their courses they fought against Sisera."[17]

"Wake up, Martha." The baritone angel voice spoke gently.

Rolling over on the soft pillowy cloud, I sighed, "Do I get to fly today?"

"What?" John's voice broke through.

"Huh?" I responded, jolting upright in bed.

"I said you'll be late for church if you don't get up soon." Carefully considering his recalcitrant wife, my husband stood beside our bed completely dressed in his Sunday best.

I quickly assessed the situation. On the one hand, Andrea Gray would be at church . . .

"Martha, did you hear me?" John seemed impatient.

"Give me a minute, will you, please?" I arranged the covers comfortably around me and burrowed into the pillows.

Without another word he vanished.

"I need to list the pros and cons," I muttered to myself. "Andrea still snipes at me, and I can't stand that anymore."

"Forgive her," a still, small voice seemed to say.

"She got her three carts, caused me untold embarrassment, and I don't want to go to church this week—maybe *never!*"

"Let us not neglect our church meetings, as some people do . . . "[18] The scriptures spoke to my soul.

By the time I'd fluffed my pillows a few times and stood in

front of the mirror staring at my shorn scalp, John and our three sons had departed. Virtue accompanied them to the sanctuary.

I, on the other hand, demoted my spiritual self-esteem to a failing mark by staying home from church. "I should have faced Andrea, but I couldn't. I'm a coward—what J.J. would call a 'wimp.' " Like a child banished for stealing cookies from the guest tray, I stood alone in my room arranging my hair stubs. "I'll never be the same again," I moaned to the mirror on the dresser.

Then I telephoned Ginny (I knew she didn't go to church). Guilt reigned supreme as I listened to her phone ring. "One . . . two . . . hello?"

"Mrs. Christian? Are you all right?" Ginny answered on the third ring.

"Of course, I am all right," I lied. "I just had some extra time on my hands and thought I'd phone to say hello."

"Really? How nice!" Her gum snapped into the receiver.

"Ginny . . ." I began.

"I knew it! There *is* something wrong. You've never phoned me at home—especially on a Sunday morning, because you always go to church on Sunday morning—"

"Ginny" I interrupted.

"Oh yes," she agreed, "you had some time on your hands and—"

"Never mind that now," I continued. "Maybe there is a little something I'd like to discuss."

"Anything at all, Mrs. Christian!"

Her words began to tumble together. "Don't get excited, Ginny," I responded smoothly. "Do you remember when that woman came to the store and helped herself to three carts?" I squinted my eyes at the memory.

"Oh, certainly!" She waited for me to continue.

"How did you happen to call the police?"

"Oh, I knew there was something wrong," she whined.

"No, no, no, Ginny," I soothed. "I meant, how did you have the foresight to phone the police?"

"Foresight?" Her voice quivered.

"Ginny, will you *relax!*"

"Yes, Ma," she replied softly.

"What I am trying to say is that I *admire* the fact that you called the police, and I am wondering how you, uh, arrived at that decision." I sat back and twirled the telephone cord.

"Oh!" her voice rose to lofty heights. "You mean, how did I get the nerve to call the cops on the stealer!" She chuckled heartily.

"Something like that," I responded nervously.

"Well, I've been taking some training on how to be *assertive*, Mrs. Christian." Her information bubbled through the telephone like a geyser getting ready to gush. "You see, I realized I shouldn't be walked on by a person trying to take something that didn't belong to her; therefore, I had to act!"

"Do you, uh, have a manual, or something to follow?"

"Oh no, Mrs. Christian, not like a war manual, if that's what you mean."

"War manual?"

"You know, like the generals. No, that's *aggression*."

"Aggression?"

"Mrs. Christian," she continued, her voice taking on a conspiratorial quality, "do you have a few minutes?"

"That's why I called, Ginny. I wasn't feeling well enough to attend church this morning, and I noticed your act of bravery at work that day, and I wondered—"

"—how you can do it too!" she pounced.

"Something like that," I answered cautiously.

"Okay, you got it, Ma. Just let me get a cup of coffee." The receiver crashed at the other end, then rumbled around on a hard surface before her lecture began. "Here's how it is, Ma." She gulped and swallowed. "You see, *aggressive* is when you are mean and hostile, and you like to hurt people, and you start wars—sort of like keepers who are cruel to their prisoners. Got it?"

"Right," I replied uneasily.

"That's what that cart-person was—aggressive."

"Yes," I agreed.

"Okay. Now we got that part." She slurped her coffee. "The next part isn't so easy."

"Of course," I interjected.

"Oh, back to the first part for a minute. My therapist—"

"This requires *therapy*?" Chills covered my forearms.

"You can call him a teacher if you want to," she comforted. "It won't make any difference. Anyway, to finish the first part—a person with *aggression* has a *closed* mind. Got it?"

"Got it."

"Now, *assertive* is when you defend yourself, and you have an open mind, and you're sort of—confident. Know what I mean? I mean, everybody has to defend herself once in a while. Why, if we didn't do that, we wouldn't have any wars!"

"I'm getting confused."

"It's not that easy, I know." She swigged another gulp of coffee. "Say, maybe you'd like to go to one of my sessions with me!"

"Ginny, I think I'm not feeling well after all. I should go and lie down. Can we keep this conversation confidential?"

"You mean secret?"

"Absolutely."

As soon as I'd replaced the receiver, I raced for the dictionary. "Hmm, *asseverate* means to assert . . ." I ran my finger along the definitions: "To *assert* is to declare, affirm, maintain, or defend rights; and to *assert oneself* means to insist on one's rights, or on being recognized!"

I hurried to the kitchen to make myself a cup of coffee. In other words, letting Andrea Gray walk all over me is to be a coward—as the kids would say, a *wimp*! I paused to let that bit of information soak in.

Suddenly I really didn't feel well. As I sat with my head in my hands at our kitchen table—not surrounded by the usual happy voices—a strange weariness washed over me.

"Lord," I whispered, "what am I going to do? Andrea Gray is just plain mean to me. Is she that way to everybody, or is it just me she can't stand?" Dropping my head, I let my shoulders slump and the tears flow.

"*Listen . . . love your enemies. Do good to those who hate you. Pray for the happiness of those who curse you; implore God's blessing on those who hurt you.*"[19] The Quiet One brought the familiar scripture to my mind.

In my mind's eye, I could see Jesus the carpenter standing on a gentle hillside, arms outstretched. It seemed to make sense.

Just then the telephone rang and I reached over to answer it.

"Martha?" John's familiar voice sounded strained.

"Anything wrong?" I inquired like a guilty child who should have gone to Sunday school but feigned sickness to stay home and play with a favorite doll.

Ignoring my question, his direct statement cut deep. "We'll be going to Andrea Gray's for Sunday dinner."

"Oh," I replied, tears stinging my eyes.

"We'll see you later then." And he was gone.

My soul tore in two as images of *my* husband and *my* children sitting down to Sunday dinner at Andrea's table flashed though my brain. "Who does she think she is!" Angrily I wiped off the telephone receiver with a dishcloth as though I could remove Andrea Gray like an unwanted germ.

Anger, like an ugly seed, planted itself in my heart, waiting to grow.

I fed it. I picked up the phone and dialed Ginny.

"Ginny?" Furiously I drummed my fingers on the counter top as I waited for my checker's voice to respond.

"Hi, Ma!" Cheerily she greeted me.

"I am interested in this assertive-thing you're talking about."

"Really?" she squealed in delight.

"How do I start?" I rubbed my eyes dry with the back of my right hand.

"Wow, Ma! This is great! Let's see—are you busy today?"

"Apparently not," I replied with a snide edge.

"Okay! You just sit tight and I'll be over in a few minutes with some info!"

While waiting for my ally to arrive, I paced back and forth in the living room. I would show that "Andy" a thing or two. I was *not* a coward, and I would *not* be a wimp! As I wore a path in our carpet, I vaguely noticed through the window a few fluffy white clouds grazing the face of the Chief, framed by an early March sky.

"Hmpf!" I groused, "they say clouds have a silver lining. Do they? Well, some of them have brass knuckles!"

Half an hour later I sat across the dining room table from Ginny. "More tea?" Picking up our china teapot, I poised it over my ally's cup.

Sticking out her cup, she watched as I accidentally filled it too full.

"Oh, excuse me!" Flustered, I grabbed the teacup and saucer. The tea rocked back and forth for a moment before exploding into the saucer. "Oh!" Quickly setting the saucer on my best tablecloth, I watched the amber liquid seep over the edge and spread a tan ring around the saucer. "Oh, I *am* sorry!"

Like a Cheshire cat, Ginny settled back and grinned. "You've got nuthin' to be sorry about, Ma."

"What?" I mopped my damp brow with my napkin.

"It's *your* tablecloth! You can spill all over it if you want to. I'll show you how. First, hold up your cup."

"It's full, Ginny."

"So much the better. Now hold it up," she commanded.

Dutifully I lifted my teacup and saucer up.

With a flair my instructor poised the pot high over the pro-posed target. A golden glow glided down from the spout toward my cup.

Fascinated, I watched the liquid fill, and then overflow into the saucer. Eyes wide and holding my breath, I waited for the inevitable to happen.

"There!" Ginny pronounced, setting the cup and saucer down on the table without spilling a drop.

"There, what?" I responded.

"There is your first lesson, Ma," she coached.

Dropping my head, I stared at my tea.

"Lesson *two*," she continued, "begins now. Start again." Lift-ing the teapot lid, she deftly dumped the contents of our cups and saucers back into the pot. Then she held her cup out to me.

Like a first-time paratrooper, I stared at the void of emptiness and recoiled in fear. "I can't, Ginny."

My instructor sighed deeply. "This is going to take longer than I expected."

"Excuse me a moment, will you, please?" Hurrying from the room, I felt pressure in my throat. "It's too much stress," I advised myself, running water in the kitchen to muffle my embarrassment.

"Whatcha doin', Mrs. Christian?" Ginny's thin voice wafted into my hearing.

"Getting a drink of water," I quickly decided. "Want one?" I gulped down a glass of water and turned off the tap.

"That's okay!" She yelled back. "I'm not thirsty!" Facing the ordeal, I returned to the table and sat down.

"Good!" My advisor began again. "All right. Let's try another one." She straightened her stiff blond hair. "Pretend I . . ." Her eyes rolled to the ceiling for inspiration. ". . . I, uh, *insult* you." Her

"Okay," I replied.

"No!" Ginny jumped up from the table. "It is *not* okay! No one should be insulted."

"I can't do this, Ginny." My nose drooped down to the table. My best grocery checker's eyes transformed themselves into pools of pleading.

Folding my arms across my chest, I put on a stern look and said, "It's only tea, and, if you insult me, I'll just feel hurt and that never solves anything."

Ginny shook her head hard from side to side. "No, Ma, you have to do better than that! People will walk all over you!"

Andrea Gray flashed across my brain. Her insults stung afresh, her sarcasm ripped my inferiority complex, and my roundness felt larger than ever as I recalled her slim figure.

"Well?" Ginny gazed expectantly at me.

"You're right, of course." My hands wrung themselves out to dry, and my nose itched violently. Nervously I rubbed it with the back of my wrist.

"Ma, dear, dear Ma." Ginny's eyes deplored my ineptness.

"My mother always said sticks and stones could break my bones, but words could never hurt me." I began folding the tablecloth into even pleats.

"But now you know that's not true, don't you?" Ginny leaned forward in her chair.

"I still can't say something mean for no reason, even if somebody else is saying mean things for no reason, Ginny." Sadly I lifted my eyes to meet her accusing gaze.

My teacher, confidant, aide, and ally changed tactics. "Look at it this way." She shoved the teacups aside. "Say somebody says, 'You're gaining weight—aren't you?' You simply turn around and say, 'You're getting a little crass—aren't you?' "

The back door slammed downstairs. "Ginny, it's my family!"

"So?" She inspected a broken fingernail. "Do you happen to have a small pair of scissors?"

"Quick! Look like we're doing nothing." Hastily I straightened the cups, saucers, and teapot.

John's step sounded heavy coming up the stairs.

Guiltily, I glued myself to my chair.

"Martha?" his deep voice sounded.

"Here, John," I called back.

In a moment he stood beside the dining room table.

"Hi, Mr. Christian!" Ginny grinned broadly. "Do you happen to have a small pair of scissors?"

My husband's puzzled expression spanned the ages. "I think Martha can probably find you a pair, uh—"

"I'm Virginia," she responded, filling in the blank.

"Yes," he replied, throwing a meaningful glance at me.

"She works for me at Kleaver's," I responded like a trained monkey. "She just dropped in for tea."

"I'll leave you two alone then," he said tonelessly just before he disappeared.

Ginny shook her head sadly. "Mrs. Christian, we've got our work cut out for us."

"Just give me some of your notes, Ginny, and I'll read them on my own."

"Oky-doky," she replied with a shrug, stuffing some papers into my hands. "But you'd learn faster if I took you to my therapist—I mean *teacher*."

By the time Ginny departed for her house, John, John Jr., Joe, and George had found ways to spend what was left of Sunday. I, on the other hand, answered the telephone, cleaned up after the dog, fed the bird, and readied myself for Monday morning.

Stashing Ginny's notes under the sheets in the linen closet, I promised myself I would read them later. Monday morning, bright and early, I stood staring at myself in the bathroom mirror. "Martha, my dear," I addressed myself, "what you need is *diversion*." Carefully arranging my hair stumps, I continued. "Today we will corral Fred to begin spring cleaning at Kleaver's!"

An hour later, Fred wilted before my gaze. "But, Mrs. Christian! That's woman's work!"

"Nonsense, Fred," I replied cheerily. "In this day and age work is not sexist—it's just *work*, and in this case, Kleaver's is a mess of untidiness." I waved my hand about the store as I marched through my office door and down the aisles.

"But we sweep the floors and mop them every day, Ma," he whined.

"Oh no, Fred, my dear, my boy!" I thumped him heartily on his back. "I don't mean clean, as in scrubbing clean; I mean clean as in *rearrange, reorganize, revitalize!*"

"Oh, well, I guess that's *different*," he mumbled, following me through the store to the stockroom.

"It will be fine, Fred," I assured, making notes as we went along. "You'll see." Glancing up at the ceiling, I sang out, "Ah, ha! I knew it! Do you see that, Fred?"

"See what?" He rolled his hazel eyes toward the top of the room.

"There's no smoke alarm in here!" Pulling a pencil stub from behind my right ear, I made a note of it.

"Oh, yeah, sure, Ma! I see it now! No smoke alarm!" He bobbed his head up and down in agreement.

"That's the spirit of cooperation we need to be a team around here, Fred. After all, Mr. Kleaver won't be sick forever, and we want his place of business to be shipshape when he returns, don't we?"

"Right, Ma! Want me to order them today?"

"Immediately, Fred, my young friend! Not only will we plan ahead and protect the future, we will be warned in the present if something is wrong." Still gesticulating, I wandered happily back to my office.

"This is terrific," I commented to myself. "I haven't felt so good in weeks." I took out a stack of clean white paper, and poised my pen.

Then I laid it down on my desk blotter and thought aloud. "I wonder if Deborah ordered the supplies for the ten thousand men from the tribes of Naphtali and Zebulun? I'm certain chariots would have needed paint at the very least . . .

"But I digress. My list awaits!" Picking up my pen, I continued talking to myself as I wrote.

"Let's see, I'll call it, 'Necessary Repairs.' Number one: Install five smoke alarms, including one outside the front door for good measure. Two: Refurbish restrooms." I scratched my head in concentration. "No, *renovate* sounds better—more specific. Yes. Renovate restrooms (paint the ladies' room pink). Number three: Get the heating system and the cooling system serviced and, if necessary, repaired. Maybe I should call them the *furnace* and the *air conditioning*.

"I need a drink of water."

I scurried to the small refrigerator Mr. Kleaver kept in his office, poured myself a glass of cold water, then hurried back to my desk.

"Number four: Trim the shrubs in front of the store and plant flowers. Number five: Check the roof for leaks and organize repairs of same." My right hand began to sweat. "My, my, why did Mr. Kleaver leave all this undone?"

Three days later, I sat exhausted in my office and said with a moan, "What do you mean Kleaver's needs a *new roof*?"

The tall contractor stood on the other side of my desk.

"Lady, you'll have to take my word for it, unless, of course you want to climb up on the roof with me and see for yourself." He folded his arms and waited.

"I don't really have time to go up on the roof," I responded timidly.

"Just let me handle it, and you'll get a good job done." He pulled out a clipboard and wrote something down.

Perspiration formed along my hairline as I remembered Ginny's advice to use short sentences and make myself plain. "Why haven't I taken time to read the rest of her notes?"

"Say something, ma'am?" The giant stopped writing.

Forcing my mouth to move, I said, "How much?"

Slowly the man in charge closed his clipboard, leaned forward across my desk, and stated, "Too soon to tell."

"Too soon?"

"We'll do a good job for you and bill you. Don't worry about a thing. We'll start tomorrow." In two strides he disappeared out of my office.

But I did worry.

The following day five smoke alarms were installed, and the bill set off at least fifty alarms in my nervous system, including an upset stomach and a blinding headache.

By the end of March, somehow Kleaver's Meats and Merchandise had acquired a new roof, five deluxe alarm devices, new vanities with fancy taps (including new floors) for the restrooms (the ladies' room wallpapered in something resembling jungle decor—complete with tropical birds in the vines), all new landscaping instead of trimmed shrubs, and an almost-new heating and cooling system for the building.

"Ginny, look at this," I moaned, handing her a sheaf of accumulated bills.

"Oh, Ma," she responded sympathetically, "how did it happen?"

"I guess I forgot to use short sentences."

"What are you going to do?" Her brown eyes betrayed misery.

Rubbing the back of my right hand across my mouth I replied, "Go to my office." As I reached my office the telephone clamored for my attention.

"Hello?" I rubbed my tired eyes and hoped to hear a friendly voice.

"Martha?" Shivers ran up my spine.

"This is Andrea!"

Yuk, I thought in a one-word sentence.

"Hello, Andrea, I was just thinking about you."

"Really? I find that difficult to believe."

"I was wondering if you ever had your hair cut," I lied to cover my embarrassment at being caught in the fib of saying I'd been thinking about her. If I'd known it was she, I wouldn't have answered the telephone in the first place.

"Not with a chain saw." She chopped at my self-esteem without mercy.

"I didn't know my hairdresser's scissors were dull. Besides, she didn't mean to cut my hair so short."

"Oh," she trilled, "did you think I meant *your* hair?"

Feeling my face flush, I couldn't respond.

"All kidding aside," she chuckled maliciously, "I called for a specific reason. I want you to hire Drulene."

Her arrogance knew no bounds. First she set me up with an insult; then she slammed me with an order. Reeling under her blows I replied, "Who is Drulene?"

Silky smooth, her voice coursed through the telephone wires and paralyzed my power to withstand her pushiness. "You see, Martha, I heard that you recently hired a young man named Fred who had no parents." I heard a sound like nails clicking on a hard surface.

"Well, yes, I did hire Fred because he was alone and sick and had nowhere to live. Actually he is doing quite well now. You would be impressed if you saw him—"

"Yes, I am certain I would, Martha," she interrupted; "that's exactly why I know you will hire Drulene."

"I will?" Confusion set in. Realizing Andrea controlled my next response didn't prevent my programmed response to her commands.

"Martha." Her voice hushed to a whisper. "My niece Drulene is nineteen years old too. She's been having a hard year at college, and she needs a little spending money."

"Spending money?"

"Now, Martha, don't start repeating what I say again. It's extremely irritating." She yawned. "Of course she needs spending money when she isn't in school."

Struggling not to repeat 'isn't in school,' I contorted my brain to come up with, "Isn't she going to school now?"

"Martha"—exasperation clipped my name to Marrr- tha—"that is why I called you—so you could give her a position at your little supermarket, which I hope, by the way, has up-graded its standards by now."

Rubbing my forehead with the fingers of my right hand, I gripped the telephone receiver more tightly. "Oh, now I understand. Drulene has quit school so she needs a job. I don't see how I can—"

"She will be there in an hour, Martha. Don't disappoint me, please."

"But we close in an hour," I pleaded.

"Exactly. That way you won't lose work time." And she hung up.

At closing time, I interviewed Drulene. After talking to her, I wondered if the college had *forced* her out.

That evening, I discussed the matter with John, who looked disinterested and replied, "Why not? Won't hurt to give her a try."

The following day in desperation, I phoned my best friend and unwavering ally. "What shall I do, Jean?"

Instead of understanding, she responded, "Why are you giving Andrea such a hard time, Martha? You know she means well . . ."

I could have asked Specimen, the dog; Buddy, the bird; or Ben, the guinea pig, but they couldn't speak English. *They are, however, my only real friends at this point,* I thought.

The next day I asked Mr. Kleaver's opinion. "Good idea, Martha. You work too hard anyway. Mrs. Gray telephoned me yesterday . . ."

Cornered, I hired Drulene. On her second day on the job I wanted to fire Drulene for her rotten attitude, snobbishness, and general laziness.

"By the way, Mrs. Christian," Drulene drawled, "Auntie Andy says you're supposed to give me a ride home tonight."

"What?" I sputtered.

"You're supposed to give me—"

"Why can't your aunt pick you up?" I retorted.

"She has an important meeting at church." Drulene whipped her hair back. "She said you'd understand."

Frustrated at my inability to stand up to Andrea, angry at

John, and wounded that my dearest friend of fifteen years would side against me—*Jean didn't even ask me what I thought*—I shoved my feelings into a corner. I retreated to my office and licked my wounds. *This is not going according to plan*, I fumed. *Deborah didn't go through this. When she fought Sisera she won—and he owned nine hundred iron chariots, not to mention the fact he'd been tormenting the children of Israel for twenty years.*[20] *Why, even the stars helped her!*

Drulene's inexperienced help counting cash resulted in our working overtime. By the time I'd turned the key in the lock, darkness had descended.

"Come on, Durlene, the car is over here."

"*Drulene*," she corrected.

"Whatever," I commented, resigned to my fate. "Look at that sky. Black as pitch. I can't see a single star."

"This looks like a good night for an accident," murmured my passenger.

"Yes." Pulling my coat around me against the cold March air, I shivered. *What a morbid thought.*

An hour later I was a casualty in our hospital's emergency room.

7 / Jael

"And Jael went out to meet Sisera, and said to him, 'Turn aside, my master, turn aside to me! Do not be afraid.' And he turned aside to her into the tent, and she covered him with a rug."[21]

"Were you wearing your seat belt?" The emergency-room nurse fogged in and out of my field of vision.

"What?" I tried to raise my arm and it fell on the narrow bed like a limp noodle.

"Your *seeet belt.*" The faceless nurse strapped a cold, dark armband on my left bicep and began making sounds like Joe pumping up his bicycle tires. "You know, a seat belt is an anchored strap that buckles across the hips to protect a passenger in case of an abrupt jarring as in an accident such as yours. Of course"—she stopped talking and placed a silver dollar made of ice on the inside of my left arm just below my elbow—"some people use shoulder straps as well."

"Shoulder?" My eyes felt heavy.

"You repeat things a lot, don't you, Mrs. Christian?" Removing the arm-constrictor, she shoved something dry into my mouth. "Now don't say anything for a moment, please. Can you sit up?"

"Umm?" I responded.

"To sign the forms," she replied matter-of-factly.

"Forms?" My head cleared enough for terror to take over.

92

"Where is John?" I hissed through teeth clenched on the thermometer.

She bustled about the small cubicle. "If you mean your husband, we haven't located him yet, but I'm certain we'll track him down soon." Removing the thermometer, she left me in my misery.

Closing my eyes, I tried to pray. "Lord, help . . ."

"Your daughter is here." The voice of another nurse broke into my headache.

"I don't have a daughter. I only have sons . . ."

"How are you feeling, Mrs. Christian?" Drulene's face appeared through my pain. "Wow, that was some accident! It was really cool! There we were right in the middle of the intersection, and that other car just roared toward us!"

"What happened?" I tried to focus my sore eyes upon the face I dreaded—the cause of my disasters—Drulene.

"You ran a red light!" She leaned upon my narrow bed on wheels, causing me excruciating pain.

"Please," I whispered, "don't touch the bed."

"Oh, sure!" Her nasal twang amplified my agony.

"Was anybody hurt?" I turned my head slowly to the left. Sharp needles ran through the back of my neck.

"Just you!" She grinned broadly. "Not a scratch on anyone else! Isn't that terrific?"

I took a deep breath. "You remind me of your Aunt Andrea."

"Do you think so?" she chirped more loudly. "I hope so because she's got her master's degree in sociology. As for me, I just flunked out this semester."

"Oh," I responded weakly.

"Mr. Christian and Aunty Andy will be here soon. I telephoned them. Lucky for us Mr. Christian was at Aunty's house. So it shouldn't be long now."

The pain in my body retreated with the torture delivered to my heart knowing that John was with Andrea Gray when I needed him most. In spite of myself, I asked, "What was he doing at your aunt's house?"

"Oh, I dunno!" she countered obliviously.

Closing my eyes, I said no more. Moments later, John and Andrea arrived.

"Martha?" John's familiar voice, which usually brought joy, stirred discomfort. "How are you feeling?"

Opening my eyes, I looked from him to Andrea, then back again. Anger, humiliation, and insult forced my mouth to stay shut.

"Was she wearing a seat belt?" The safety nurse had arrived.

John took my limp hand in his and held it. "I wasn't with her," he responded.

The warmth of his hand soothed me enough to pry open my lids again and look at my spouse.

"Who was with her?" The person in hospital garb held up her clipboard with pencil ready.

"My niece," Andrea Gray offered confidently.

Finally I could stand it no longer. Turning my eyes to John, I said, "What difference does it make whether or not I wore my seat belt?"

"You bumped your head, Martha. Maybe they want to know how hard."

"Oh," I replied, happy to have him near. "That's funny. I can't remember."

"Excuse me, everyone," a bearded young man announced, pushing his way into the small area. "X-rays."

Soon he and two other orderlies sped me down the halls to a room that smelled a little like old tires.

"My head hurts," I complained, "and my stomach feels sick."

Ignoring me, they took pictures of my head and neck, then returned me to my cubicle in the emergency room.

Since Drulene sustained no injuries, Andrea took her home.

Alone with John, I confided, "This never would have happened if Andrea hadn't pushed me into hiring Drulene and then expected me to take her home!"

"Martha, it's nobody's fault. Accidents happen." He gently patted my hand.

"Did I run the red light?"

"Everyone seems to think you did."

"I don't think I did," I retorted, pulling my hand away. My

brain received word of the effort, and pain pulsed through my head. A white coat appeared between the dark green curtains of my compartment.

"Why, Mrs. Christian!" a male voice sang. The blue eyes behind tinted lenses twinkled. "Weren't you a Smock Lady here last year?"

"Yes, I was, but I don't remember—"

"Don't worry about a thing, Martha!" He turned his attention to John. "We would like to keep her overnight for observation."

Another rolling bed arrived and pushed its way through the curtains.

"But, what about—"

"You just leave the driving to us, Martha. You're going to be just fine. It's only a precaution."

Later, I lay alone in my bed and tried not to cry. Crying would only make my head hurt worse.

A young nurse's aide popped her head into my room and asked, "How are you feeling?"

"Terrible," I replied as cheerfully as I could. She disappeared. A while later I managed to doze off.

"Mrs. Christian?" A mountain of a nurse pulled out my arm and began wrapping it with the blood pressure cuff again. "Put this in your mouth, please."

"My head really hurts and I think I'm going to be sick."

Without a word she straightened her back, removed the pressure contraption, dropped a kidney basin on my chest, and departed.

I wondered what time it was. Straining to see through the closed hospital curtains, I drifted into a dreamless sleep.

Another face appeared, and under it, a tray laden with instruments. "Your arm, please."

A sharp needle punctured my arm, removing some of my lifeblood.

"What's that for? I was in an accident—I'm not sick!"

"Just orders," the voice monotoned before leaving.

Unable to keep my eyes open, I passed into the land of Nod for what seemed like thirty seconds.

"Wake up, Mrs. Christian," another face ordered.

"Why? It's night. Don't we sleep at night?"

"It will be time for breakfast soon. You need to wash your face." She handed me a lukewarm, damp washcloth and stood guard while I attempted to wipe sleep away.

After that I gave up trying to drift off. "They don't seem to care how bad my head hurts," I commented, pushing the kidney basin down by my left knee. "At least somebody could tell me what's going on, couldn't they?"

It felt as if two hours passed before my breakfast tray appeared. "Mrs. Christian!" The tiny nurse seemed to recognize me.

Staring intently at the young woman in front of me, a name flashed in my mind. "Sherry?"

"Yes, of course, Sherry!" She danced my tray over and set it down on my serving table. "I was a nurse's aide when you were a Smock Lady. Don't you remember?"

"Yes, I do." A grin creased my cheeks. "You got me to empty all the bedpans."

"Not *all*," she said with a smile.

"Can you tell me anything about what's wrong with me?"

"Here's breakfast!" She lifted the covers from the dishes to reveal yellow jiggling gelatin, a slimy white paste, and dry toast. A cup of hot water and a caffeine-free tea bag completed the meal. I closed my eyes against the sight.

"Now, Mrs. Christian, you know you have to eat," she gently chided.

"That's not food," I replied, turning my head away.

"You want to go home, don't you?"

"Yes, but—"

"That settles it then. I'll be back in a few minutes." She sailed toward the door. "Don't disappoint me . . ." And she vanished like the sun dropping beneath the sea at dusk.

Propping myself up on one elbow, I tried the yellow gelatin first. "Lemon! Why lemon in the morning?" I said to myself.

"To put a smile on your face!" Replied a bearded physician who suddenly appeared beside my bed.

"Are you going to tell me anything about my condition?"

"Yes, Mrs. Christian, I am." Folding his arms across his chest, he planted his feet squarely on the floor beside my bed. "Your X-rays are all right. You have a mild concussion, which explains your headache, and some possible nerve damage in your neck, but that should heal with time."

"How much time?" I narrowed my eyes in suspicion.

"Difficult to say, but you can go home today and see your own doctor in a week to set up physical therapy." He turned to leave.

"Wait a minute!" I held out my arm in his direction as though wishing it could restrain him.

"Yes?" He paused at the doorway.

"I work! I mean, I manage a supermarket—Kleaver's Meats and Mer—maybe you've heard of it . . ."

His blank stare revealed he hadn't.

"Anyway, I have to go back to work. The owner, Mr. Kleaver, had a heart attack, and he can't come back yet . . ." My speech slowed to a stop when I realized he wasn't interested in my problems. "What will I do?" Tears filled my eyes.

"Get someone to take your place," he responded flatly before melting into the hall never to be seen again.

By late afternoon, John had deposited me at home, and the kids had arrived one by one to offer condolences and to ask, "What's for supper, Mom?"

Once the din died down, I asked my dearest friend in all the world—my husband and mate for life—the question that tormented me more than the injury to my head and neck. "John, what will I do about Kleaver's?"

He kissed me softly on my forehead and smoothed the hair back from my bruised face. "I'll ask Andy, Martha. Maybe Drulene can take over for you."

"What!" I raised my voice, which in turn set off a booming within my skull. "If I hadn't been taking Drulene home, I wouldn't be tied to this bed while she's running around perfectly fine!"

"Accidents happen, Martha," my spouse sympathized, bringing a telephone beside the bed and placing it on a night table. "Drulene says you ran a red light." He busied himself shoving clothes into drawers.

"I can't believe you would believe that . . ."

"Martha, don't upset yourself. Everything is going to be fine. The boys and I have to leave for school soon. It's parents' night. I'll have to do double duty as parent and teacher since you can't go. Call if you need me."

"That's fine for *you* to say! *You're* managing to go off to *your* job. I'm just going to *lose* mine!" I stuffed my head back into my pillows and stuck out my lower lip.

Moments later, the house sounded like a tomb.

I lay in bed and stared at the ceiling.

Reaching for the telephone, I dialed Jean's number. "Hi, Jean," I intoned in misery.

"Martha!" Her cheery greeting warmed me. "How are you feeling?"

"Rotten," I replied.

"Yes, I know. Andrea called me."

A stab of ice chilled my heart. "Is that why you haven't called me?"

"I was going to check on you, but Andrea told me you needed rest, and I didn't want to bother you."

"What *else* did Andrea say?" I narrowed my eyes in suspicion.

"Only that you received a mild concussion and sustained some possible nerve damage in your neck."

"Is that *all*?"

"Yes, I guess so. Why?"

"What did *she* say about the accident?" My patience grew thin as I set myself to inspect the case of my friend versus my foe.

"Only that you were so tired you ran a red light. Why?" Her voice, usually so soothing to my system, raked across my nerves.

I wanted to scream, "Traitor!" Instead, I replied simply, "I don't know how she would know. She wasn't there."

"Martha," Jean admonished, "anyone can run a red light. It was an accident. Don't punish yourself."

"I didn't do it!" I retorted. "Drulene was talking, and that other car shot out of the intersection, and—"

"Hey, sweetie, it's me, Jean! You don't have to defend your actions to me! I love you anyway!"

"Well, it doesn't sound like it to me. Why won't you believe me? Why won't anybody believe me?" A lump formed in my throat, and my head pounded.

"Let's talk about it another day, Martha. When you're better." The tone of my best friend's voice sounded alien.

"Fine, Jean," I fibbed; "another day."

Depression drove me down into the depths of self-doubt. I lay back on the pillows and tried to rest, but my gaze caught my well-worn Bible, which John had placed beside the telephone on the night table.

That's what I need—some comfort.

Reaching across the telephone, an eerie foreboding washed over me, and I shivered. "Almost like a cold chill," I commented to myself straining to reach my Bible.

When the telephone rang just under my elbow, I jumped a foot. "Oh, the pain," I moaned, settling myself back on the bed to answer the clamor.

"Yes," I groaned into the receiver.

"Hello? Mrs. Christian?" Drulene droned into my telephone.

"What is it, Durlene?" I rubbed my eyes in frustration.

"*Dru*lene. I'm at Kleaver's. Just thought I'd help you out like Auntie Andy said, and guess what I found?"

"Found?" Goose bumps forced the hair on my arms to stand on end.

"Yeah. I found a whole pile of bills for repairs here at Kleaver's, like for a new roof, five smoke alarms, a whopping big one for air conditioning and heating"—she took a breath and continued sealing my fate—"and here's some stuff about money spent for new vanities in the ladies' restroom, and fancy taps, and a *corker* for the landscaping in front of the store!"

Nausea forced me to lie flat for the final ultimatum.

"So, I phoned Mr. Kleaver. It didn't look like you'd done anything about paying these, and Auntie always says to pay your bills as quickly as possible, or you may get thrown into debtor's prison."

I whispered, "You telephoned Mr. Kleaver?"

"Sure did! And he said he'll be phoning you right away! Anything else you want me to do?"

Closing my eyes against the world, my voice rustled through my windpipe. "You've done quite enough. Why don't you go home?"

"Nah," she shot back, "I can find lots to do here. I'll help Ginny." A flash of light broke through the dim conversation into my brain.

"Ginny? Get me Ginny."

"You want to talk to her?" Drulene figured the obvious.

"Yes!" My voice surged through my throat. "Get Ginny now!"

"Okay!" She dropped the receiver.

While waiting for Ginny to come to the phone, I pushed my throbbing brain into action.

"I need a plan," I announced to myself.

"Ma?" Ginny's voice tinkled like a bell through the telephone.

"Ginny, help me!"

"Anything, Ma! What's wrong? Is it your head?"

In my mind's eye I could see Ginny all giddy and excited. "No, Ginny, it's the *bills*—the repair bills. Drulene found them and called Mr. Kleaver, and I didn't have a chance to explain them to him."

Her hushed voice shoved shivers up my spine. "You mean those *huge* repair bills?"

Taking a deep breath, I replied, "The sky-high ones."

"Uh-oh, Ma, you're dead."

"Thanks, Ginny." My knuckles whitened as they strangled the telephone receiver. "Isn't there anything in your notes about being assertive in this situation?"

"That's a tough one, Ma. Usually you're assertive when you're being picked on."

"I *am* being picked on!"

"You know that. I know that. But Mr. Kleaver doesn't know that."

"I got a whiplash, Ginny. I know it's whiplash." Whimpering in pain, I struggled to balance my aching head on my hurting neck.

"Wow, Ma. This is tough. What are you going to do?"

"Hang up the phone and await the execution," I replied, terror forming a knot in my stomach.

No sooner had I spoken and replaced the receiver than the telephone rang loud and clear.

"Hello?" Like a tiny gray house mouse, I held the receiver in my hands close to my mouth.

"Martha, what's this I hear about some astronomical repair bills?" The voice of Mr. Kleaver divided the telephone wire into two parts—terror and defeat.

I inhaled deeply for strength. "Mr. Kleaver, I am sorry you had to hear about the bills from Drulene. I was going to explain—"

"When, Martha? Next Christmas?" My boss interrupted with never-before-used-on-me sarcasm.

Stumped, stunned, and feeling stupid, I quipped without thinking, "Do you want me to quit?"

"I'll think about it, Martha."

Wanting to apologize, but unable to grasp the rapid turn of events, I remained silent.

"When will you be back to work?" His voice, usually so gentle, grated on my ears.

"I'll try to go in tomorrow, Mr. Kleaver," I responded like a whipped dog.

"Whatever, Martha." His voice softened a bit. "We'll discuss this financial thing at a later date—when I'm back to work."

Fear clutching my stomach, I failed to gather enough nerve to inquire how soon he'd be back. Instead I said, "Thank you, Mr. Kleaver." I cried most of the day.

The next morning I couldn't go to work. Every time I stood up the room reeled around me. Mrs. Kleaver took over the store for me.

Over the next three days I turned to the book of Judges and Deborah for encouragement. What would Deborah have done? Alone in the house, reading my Bible, I gathered strength. Now I would find out what really made Deborah tick and apply it to myself.

On Friday, after everyone had left for school, I discovered

Jael. "And Jael . . . said, 'Turn aside . . . to me!' And he turned aside to her into the tent. . . . And he said to her, 'Please give me a little water to drink, for I am thirsty.' So she opened a bottle of milk and gave him a drink . . ."[22]

Sitting alone on the sofa, my heart sank to my heels. *Jael.* Instantly my mind envisioned her—tall, willowy, with raven black hair.

Unable to stop myself, I read on, "But Jael, Heber's wife . . ."

"So! Jael had a husband! I wonder what Andrea's husband—what's-his-name—thinks of John helping Andrea all the time. Poor guy. Nobody even knows who he is." I gazed into space. "Come to think of it, I think his name is Leonard. He probably comes to church with Andrea, but I've never seen her with a man—except *my* husband, that is."

"For jealousy and selfishness are not God's kind of wisdom."[23] The familiar verse quoted so often by my godly mother halted my destruction-bound train of thinking.

Picking up my Bible, I glanced again at the printed page before me. "But Jael, Heber's wife, took a tent peg and seized a hammer in her hand, and went secretly . . . and drove the peg into his temple, and it went through into the ground; for he was sound asleep and exhausted. So he died."[24]

"Oh my! Andrea, I mean *Jael* killed him!" Worry took over where marital jealousy quit. My nerves twisted into numerous knots.

Sitting alone on the sofa, I bowed my head and prayed, "Lord, help me. You know this kind of thinking should never enter a wife's head." A quiet peace settled upon my shoulders. Flipping the pages of the Lamp of my life, I found a special treasure: "Cease from anger, and forsake wrath; fret not thyself in any wise to do evil."[25]

Silent, I sat for a long time as the war within me raged. On one hand, Andrea's aggressiveness evoked my desire to retaliate. On the other hand, however, I didn't want to cross her. Did that mean I was a coward?

Pacing slowly back and forth across the living room, I reasoned, *Wonder what's on the daytime television? Usually I'm too busy to turn it on.*

Retrieving the remote control device from our TV, I settled myself in an easy chair and pushed the ON button.

"I might as well watch the idiot tube while no one can disturb me," I muttered to myself. When J.J. was home, all I saw were flashing channels as he sat and switched channels. But just for fun I held the tuning button down and watched programs fly by at warp speed. While whizzing past channels, I heard a mind-changing idea. "Do *you* hate yourself because you are *fat*?"

Screeching the buttons to a halt, I tuned in and answered, "Yes. All I am is a gray, round house mouse. Why should I have to be a short, round mound, while Andrea Gray is tall, willowy, and gorgeous to boot?"

"If you've had enough of your present lifestyle—eating cookies on the run because you're too busy to prepare proper food . . ."

"Oh yes," I agreed, nodding as much as my stiff neck allowed.

"If you stand in shame," the perfect voice and figure continued, "because you eat for *fun* . . ."

"Oh yes." I hung my head as far as I could before I winced with pain.

"If you know the *embarrassment* of refusing to stand next to someone willowy . . ."

"Oh! How did *you* know?" My eyes opened wide in amazement.

"Oh, I *know* what it's like," the perfect size-eight spoke with feeling, "because I used to weigh two hundred pounds!"

"No!" I gasped.

"Yes!" she countered.

For the next forty-five minutes, I sat cemented to my spot on the sofa. At the closing credits, I knew what I had to do. "I am going on a diet!"

Hope surged life anew in my system. I hurried through the house carrying a garbage bag. "I will search out and destroy every fat-producing goody in the house! She's right," I muttered, grabbing some expensive salted nuts and dropping them in the plastic sack without a backward glance. "I am what I eat! I eat junk! Therefore, I am—"

I couldn't bring myself to say the word.

By the time I'd twisted the tie on the trash bag, virtuous feelings flooded through my brain. "This is incredible! I feel thinner already. Gone are the nuts, chocolates, chips, and other crunchies! They're pure poison. I *know* I'll never miss them."

"And," I reasoned as I ran down the basement stairs with the sack—to burn calories, "since I work in a grocery store, I have easy access to fresh, ripe, wholesome produce!"

Realizing that thinking thin, eating salads, and increasing exercise would create a new Martha, my spirits soared as I prepared dinner. Lightheartedly I chopped, washed, peeled, and steamed all the healthful foods I had on hand. Singing overcame the growling of my rebellious stomach, and I conquered all hunger pangs.

"Supper is ready!" I shouted to the family now assembled in our house.

"There's no food on the table, Mom." John Jr. appeared first. John sat down at the head of the table.

"Great! Supper!" Joe and George chorused.

With great ceremony I moved around my children and set a covered dish before the king of our castle. "*Voilà!*"

"What's this?" John's face fell when I lifted the white china cover to reveal a mass of steaming green.

"Yuk! Argh!" George and Joe bounced around the table coughing and sputtering as though looking upon wholesome food would poison them.

"As I said, Mom," John Jr. stood up and pushed his chair back, "there's no food on the table."

"It's good for you," I replied amiably, returning to the kitchen for more steaming vegetables. "Soon you may even *like* it!"

When I returned, the dining room was empty.

"Oh, well," I comforted myself, "tomorrow I will start them on bran for breakfast."

Once the boys and their father returned from the local hamburger house, I approached John. "How could you?"

"Easy," he replied kissing me. "How 'bout you? Want a hamburger with all the trimmings?"

"Most certainly not, John." I tilted my nose in the air. "Someday you will thank me for caring about our health."

"Not today though, Martha. I'm not sick." With that remark he departed to the back of the house.

"Hey, Mom?" John Jr. appeared with mustard around his mouth. "Remember Babs?" His eyes told the story of young love in bloom.

How could I forget the five-foot-two-eyes-of-blue bombshell who had stolen my son's heart and then moved out of town? "You've been writing her for months, J.J. Of course I remember."

"She's moving back, Mom." He took a deep breath and puffed out his manly chest. *"Here!"*

8 / Smog

"Then war was in the gates. Not a shield or spear was seen among forty thousand in Israel."[26]

"One, two, three, four, and *kick*! Pause! Now, left side. One, two, three, four, and *kick*!" Television's Twig-Lady demonstrated the way to the thin life right in the privacy of my own home.

"One, two three, four and *ouch*!" I tried my best to follow and failed. "How come my leg only lifts a foot off the floor?"

"All together now! Kick! Kick! Kick!" Edith Exercise nimbly danced and shouted simultaneously.

"Ow! Ow! Ow! Ow!" I puffed, in the middle of my living room. Flopping down on the rug, I lay back and tried to catch my breath. "I'm probably going to have a heart attack on top of whiplash," I gasped.

"Now! Get down on all fours with your hands and knees about eight inches apart," announced Edith.

"Don't you ever get winded?" I narrowed my gaze suspiciously. "Maybe you're not even real."

"Ah, ah," she crooned, "we have some people sitting down instead of kneeling for our next exercise . . ."

"All right. All right," I muttered to our TV. "I'm going to do it right now." Using all my remaining strength, I forced my body to bended knees. "Now what?"

"Now! Raise your right leg and kick it back as far as it will go!"

I watched in fascination as the slim, trim body expert picked up her knee while still in a crouch and effortlessly shoved it out behind her, toe pointing to the ceiling. Very carefully I picked up my right leg. "So far so good," I commented. Somehow the movement used to throw my leg out behind me shoved me over on my side, and I landed in a heap on the floor.

"Now! Left side!"

"I haven't got the right side yet!"

Totally frustrated, I sat back and waited for an easier exercise.

After a few more minutes of kneeling, pulling her right knee up, kicking her right leg back and out; then pulling her right leg in under to try to force her right knee to the middle of her chin, Edith prepared me (and the other ladies all over the country crazy enough to participate in this sort of thing in the morning all alone while the rest of the family went to school and work) for the next bone-breaker.

"All right! That was terrific! Now for our next exercise, I want you to sit on the floor and face the television screen."

"Amen to *sit*!" Pulling myself together, I sat like an Indian ready to sign a peace treaty.

"Back straight?" Edith's blue eyes smiled encouragement.

Sitting as straight as I could, I balanced myself with my hands on either side of me and shoved my legs out in front. "This will be great, I hope." Staring expectantly at the screen, I waited for Edith's direction.

"Put the soles of your feet together, like this." Edith smacked the soles of her limber tootsies together in one move.

Letting go of the floor beside me, I managed to position my feet so the bottoms met each other.

"Got it?"

"Yes."

"All right! Now, simply pull your two feet together toward your body like this!" With one move she turned into a person with legs like a frog.

Grabbing my ankles, I struggled to keep my feet together.

"Ready for the next move?"

"No!"

"Terrific!"

"Wait!"

"Maybe I should give you another minute."

"Thank you," I groaned, pulling my feet a little closer to the rest of me.

"Okay! Time's up! Now, here's what we do! Put your right hand on your right knee, and your left hand on your left knee—"

"Makes sense," I interjected.

"Now shove your knees to the floor! One, two, three, four, five, six, seven, eight, nine, and ten!"

Like a rabbit frozen by a bright light at night, I sat and stared as her loose limbs bent flat to the exercise mat.

Timidly pushing on my knees, I felt excruciating pain shoot into my hip sockets.

"No pain. No gain!" Happily she counted and moved her frog legs to the rhythm of suitable leg-breaking music.

"Now! Let's take a break!"

"Good," I moaned; "even my eyes hurt."

Pulling myself up on my feet, I hurried out the kitchen for some sustenance. "What I wouldn't give for a doughnut right about now." Closing my eyes, I pictured the kind of doughnut my great aunt made when I was a little girl—crisp on the outside, tender on the inside, and covered in pure white powdered sugar. "It was the lard, I'm certain of it. Frying them on the wood stove in lard."

From the kitchen I heard Edith calling, "Next exercise!"

"I don't care. I want a doughnut fried in lard," I responded rebelliously.

"One, two, three, and—"

"All right! I won't eat anything!" Turning on my toes, I attempted a pirouette and hit the kitchen table. "Ow," I mumbled in pain.

By the time Edith Exercise terminated the lesson, I felt finished as a human being. "Fat! That's what I am, and there is absolutely no point in calling myself pleasingly plump, or cute, or delicately overweight, or a couple of pounds too heavy. I am *fat!*"

Turning off the television, I headed for the kitchen cupboards. "There must be something white around here to eat. If

I see another plate of green, or dark brown, I'll die. Why does all the thin stuff have to be yellow, green, or brown? Why not something pure white . . ." I paused for a moment as a delightfully delicious idea crossed my brain. "Marshmallows! Yes! We have marshmallows! I know we do because I always hide them from George!" Like a streak of light I flew to the hall closet where I hid the luscious white things.

"None!" Eyes wide open in horror, I could not believe my son had outsmarted me. Defeated, I trudged back to the kitchen and put water on for decaffeinated coffee.

A few minutes later, I sat sipping the black beverage. "With no sugar. Yuk. Life is not going to be worth living without sugar," I complained to my audience of one.

Sitting by myself, I could see in my mind's eye a marshmallow toasting over an open fire, and me at the other end of the stick waiting to enjoy the tempting treat. "This is ridiculous. I don't even like marshmallows. I must be dieting too hard. George is the one who drools over the grocery sacks, hoping to catch a glimpse of a marshmallow."

My mind drifted to our family picnics when the children were small. The gentle breezes, the warmth of a crackling fire, and the faces of my family floated before my eyes. "Memories are precious," I decided, rinsing my coffee cup. "I remember the first time John Jr. brought Babs to one of our picnics. I felt a mixture of pride in his growing up and a sense of loss, knowing that I was not the only woman in his life anymore. At fifteen, Barbara Murrey stood five-feet-two-inches tall—all dynamite. Completely boy-crazy, her rambunctiousness, coupled with her long blond hair framing bright blue eyes, struck terror in my mother's heart.

Walking over to the window to view the Chief, I remarked to the blue-tailed bird, Buddy, "Wasn't I silly? Why, she's moved away and . . ."

A jolt hit my nervous system. "Didn't J.J. say she's coming back?"

The silence of the house surrounded me.

Goose bumps broke out all over my arms and ankles. "He did say she'd be back, but when?"

I bent over and touched my toes. "But don't be silly, Martha," I advised. "John Jr. has forgotten all about Babs because of Laura."

I stretched my arms toward the living room ceiling. "Yes, Laura should balance that situation nicely. . . ."

While standing in front of the window relaxing, I thought I saw a wisp of smoke float past.

"That's funny. I don't smell anything." Instantly alert, I hurried from room to room as fast as my multiple bruises would allow, looking for a fire.

No fire.

Back at the living room window, I opened it a crack and sniffed. "What is that foul odor? It smells like burning rubber!"

Shoving the window open, I stuck my head out and saw black smoke arising from Mrs. O's backyard.

"What's this? It looks as if smoke is coming from that contraption they've built!"

The black cloud puffed, reduced itself to a wisp, and disappeared.

"I must be imagining things," I comforted. "She's probably burning a few leaves to get ready for gardening. After all, it is May."

"That's a good idea—spring cleaning. I'll begin tomorrow and whip the house into shape before I return to work."

A goal put purpose into my steps as I vacuumed and dusted my way through the house.

While dusting J.J.'s desk, I couldn't help but notice the open letter from Babs lying on top of his history book. "Love you lots, Babs," jumped off the page.

Immediately I remembered the circumstances of her leaving.

Babs' mother and father had separated because Mrs. Murrey hadn't wanted to quit her job to move when her husband had received a transfer.

"Babs showed remarkable maturity looking after her nine-year-old brother Johnny during that troublesome time," I said while watering plants.

"Anyway, it worked out well. Finally they all went to be together." I filled the sprinkling can and put a few drops of plant food into the water and watched it turn green. "Wonder why they're moving back here?"

Moving around the house loosened up my muscles to the point of renewed energy. "Guess I'll wash the curtain sheers tomorrow morning bright and early."

Supper surprised John. "Hamburgers? We get fattening hamburgers? With french fries?"

"Don't tell her, Dad," Joe chimed in. "Maybe she's had a lapse of memory."

"Yeah, Dad," George jumped in, "she might change her mind!" Shoving his glasses higher on his nose by wiggling his face, George's braces gleamed through his broad grin. "Great, Mom! Terrific!"

"George, my dear," I leaned forward on my elbows, "I have something to discuss with you after dinner."

"Sure, Mom! Why not now?"

"Marshmallows, George."

"Great, Mom! For dessert! I love 'em." He chomped a large bite out of his burger.

"They're missing, George."

George's blue eyes gazed steadily at me. "Why?"

"George, you know why."

"No, I don't."

"Don't lie to me, George." I frowned in warning.

"I'm *not* lying, Mom!" George yelled.

"Martha, I thought you said you'd discuss this after supper." John flashed a look of irritation my direction.

"John, you don't seem to understand that somebody stole marshmallows from the hall closet!"

"What are they doing in the hall closet?" John's eyebrows went up.

"Never mind *what* they are doing there because they aren't there anymore, which is the point of this whole discussion, John." I clenched my teeth.

"Martha"—John laid his hamburger down on his plate, ready to do battle—"we do not argue at the table, if you can recall that agreement which has stood for a number of years."

"John"— I stuffed a french fry into my mouth and bit down

hard—"I specifically stated I wished to discuss this after supper; if your ears are open, then hear it."

"Then drop it." John glared at me.

Just then J.J. arrived at the supper table. "What's the hassle, Mom?"

"Why are you late for supper again, John Jr.?" I snapped through three fried potatoes.

"What's the problem, Mom?" J.J. slumped down in his chair and poured catsup all over his plate.

I took another bite of my burger.

"What's wrong, Dad? How come Mom won't talk to me?" My oldest son took command of the situation.

"Your mother can't find the marshmallows in the hall closet," John remarked dryly.

"That's cuz I took them," he remarked, squirting mustard on his hamburger.

"You what?" I interjected.

"I was hungry, Mom. You haven't been feeding us too well lately, you know." His blue teenage eyes challenged me.

I dropped my gaze to my plate. "I'll get dessert," I said.

"How come it's okay for J.J. to steal marshmallows?" whined George.

"It's not okay," I responded, setting bowls for ice cream on the table.

"I would have had to stay in my room for a week!" George stuck out his upper lip and crossed his arms.

John said nothing.

I began slapping ice cream into bowls and passing them around the table.

"That stinks!" George shouted. "And it's *unfair* too!"

"Cool it, George," Joe chimed.

Like an armed camp we finished our meal.

Bright and early the next morning I carefully removed the white sheer drapes from the living room window and popped them into the washing machine.

"Cleanliness is next to godliness," I quipped, dusting off a few basement rafters. "If only my sinuses didn't hurt so much with all the spring pollens around, I'd paint the kitchen today too."

The telephone rang, and I ran up the stairs. "Running up these stairs will get me in shape. I wonder if Deborah was fat?"

Picking up the receiver, I sang, "Hello!"

"Got a cold?"

"No, Jean, stuffed spring sinuses for sale."

"I heard Babs is coming back."

"How did you know?"

"Andrea Gray called me this morning."

"How did she find out?"

"Didn't you tell her?"

"Jean, I have to go. I'm trying to get my white sheers out on the line before it gets any later." I hoped my disappointment in her finding out about Babs from *Andrea* didn't show.

"You upset about anything, Martha?"

"Don't be silly, Jean. I'm just in a hurry."

"I'll talk to you tomorrow then," she warmly replied.

"I'll be pretty busy over the weekend, and then I'll be going back to work on Monday."

"Oh."

"I'll talk to you some day next week."

"How are you feeling since the accident?"

"Fine. I really have to go, Jean."

"Certainly, Martha. Didn't mean to make you late."

My heart turned to ice as I hung up the phone. I'd been unkind to Jean, and I knew it. For years we'd talked every day if only for a couple of minutes. "Oh, well, she can call Andrea," I said, heading back to the washing machine.

The bright morning sunshine chased my blues as I stretched as high as possible to reach the clothes line. "Ah, pure white curtains. They will not only look clean, they'll freshen the entire house with spring!"

After carefully pinning the curtains, I stopped to smell the fresh air and check out the Chief. "Nothing so lovely as sunshine sparkling on the mountaintop. Think I'll bake some cookies!"

Hurrying up the basement stairs, I heard a still, small voice say, "A man of many friends comes to ruin, but there is a friend who sticks closer than a brother."[27]

"I should have been nice to Jean." My feet headed toward the telephone. "She is my dearest friend. Why should it bother me that she talks to Andrea?"

I dialed her number.

No answer.

"Huh, she's probably at Andrea Gray's right now." A green-eyed monster darkened my vision. "Well, if that's what she wants to do with her time, so be it."

Baking cookies always relaxed me when I was upset. I should have realized something was wrong when I baked three hundred cookies nonstop.

Three hours later, I wiped my brow with the back of a floured hand. "There! That should keep everyone happy around here, and I can freeze some for next week while I'm at work too."

I should have felt happy, but I didn't. For one thing, I ate a pile of the cookies. "A moment on the lips—forever on the hips," I groaned.

And then, I felt bad about Jean. "I know I'm being dishonest. I should admit to Jean that Andrea Gray is trying to destroy my life. Probably she would understand."

A purple-eyed ugly distrust-thing colored my view.

"On the other hand, maybe she would take Andrea's side against me. That would end our friendship of many years, and I don't think . . ."

My thought processes were interrupted by the smell of smoke. "What's that foul odor?" Quickly I glanced at the oven. "It's off," I noted mentally.

Tilting my head to the side I sniffed, stood still, and listened for the crackling sound of fire.

"That's strange," I said, wiping my hands on a towel. Hurriedly I checked the house.

When I reached the living room, my eyes could not believe what they saw. "Smoke! Huge clouds of smoke! All coming from Mrs. O's backyard and heading straight for . . ."

I ran to the living room window and opened it. ". . . for my freshly washed white curtains!"

Slamming the window shut, I coughed. "That smell is terrible! I'll speak to Mrs. O right now just like Ginny says."

I stormed down the basement stairs, huffing and puffing all the way. "Why, I'll just tell her we can't have this because I do my spring cleaning in May. How can she be so thoughtless?"

Whipping open the basement door, I rushed outside. "Oh, dear! Just look at my drapes! They're gray!" Grabbing them from the clothes line, I hurried into the house and threw then back into the washing machine, added some soap powder, and flipped on the switch.

Once the suds piled high in the washer, I turned my attention to the source of the smoke—my neighbor, Mrs. O.

"Let's see now, Ginny said it's assertive to tell the truth, present my case, and not allow myself to be a runway. Furthermore, I will need to establish two-way communication, and openly mention the offending behavior." My mood lightened a little. "Maybe this will give me practice in learning how to assert myself against Andrea Gray!"

With hope in my heart, and a speech poised on my lips, I headed out the door and across the lawn in search of Mrs. O.

"Is anybody here?" I walked along our side of the fence while peering through shrubs and trees, trying to see inside her yard.

No Mrs. O, and the smoke shrank to a thin, black line.

Curiosity overcame caution as I strained my eyes to see the small building with a smokestack on top. "Hmm," I said to a nearby tree, "wonder what in the world this thing is for?" Just as I stood there, Mrs. O emerged from the little door leading to the small building that looked like a playhouse.

Startled, I shrieked, "Oh!"

"Oh!" she replied in kind. Just then the smokestack belched black, foul-smelling fog.

Plastering a smile on my face to cover my shock at realizing the contraption was a garbage incinerator, I coughed noticeably. "How's it going?"

"Huh?" My neighbor spoke a new language.

Pointing to the offending pollution device, I tried another tactic. "This is May."

"Uh huh," she drawled in disinterest.

"In May," I carefully continued, "I do my spring cleaning."

"Uh huh."

"That means you must stop burning trash in your incinerator."

"Uh huh."

Suddenly anger born of prejudice against all two-syllable-speaking peoples of the world burst out of my mouth. "I said you must stop! That's spelled s-t-o-p!" Wildly I gestured with my hands, raising the volume of my voice for clarity. "Stop! Like a stop sign at the corner when you drive your car!"

Her gaze never wavered.

Feeling like a lunatic, I yelled, "You do drive a car, don't you?"

"Uh huh," she answered, folding her arms across her chest.

"Now we're getting somewhere," I announced, lowering the volume and pitch of my discourse. "I am going back inside my house now, and I demand you stop burning trash!" Without waiting for her final rebuttal, I stomped back across our yard and into the basement.

"Well, I guess I asserted myself that time," I muttered to myself, pulling the freshly washed drapes from the washer. "Now I can hang these, and we can go on with living."

Opening the basement door, I could not believe my eyes as gigantic clouds of black erupted from the smokestack, covering our entire backyard. "Why, this will kill all the plants—maybe even the grass!"

Fury rendered me speechless as I stood watching our yard disappear in the offending fog. "Why, I never! The nerve!"

Turning around, I marched back into the basement. "How could she!"

An hour later, I stood staring out our picture window at the smoke. Anger burned and I wanted revenge.

The Still Quiet One made a few references to vengeance belonging to the Lord, but I couldn't be bothered. I tuned myself out from peace and got ready to make war. "Deborah went to war, didn't she?"

I didn't bother to remember that Deborah was *asked* to accompany Barak—"Then Barak said to her, 'If you will go with me, then I will go; but if you will not go with me, I will not go.' "[28]

Over the next day and a half, the idea and smell of smoke consumed my every waking hour until I felt compelled to deal with the situation. "But what can I do?" The powerlessness of my dilemma forced me to retreat within myself. "If I ask John what he thinks, he'll just tell me not to worry about it." Friday became Saturday. Still the smoke erupted at will, blackening my world. "I can't even see the Chief with all that smog."

I considered reporting a fire next door, but thought better of it.

"There must be a zoning law!" Reaching for the telephone, I called city hall.

"You have reached city hall. Our hours are Monday to Friday from 8:00 A.M. to 4:00 P.M. If you would like to leave a message, please begin after the tone. Beep."

Slamming down the receiver in disgust, I paced the floor. "There's got to be a way to stop her from creating that smog!"

From the back of the house, I heard sounds of a scuffle and Joe's voice, "Get him out!"

Hurrying toward the noise, I saw Joe standing in the middle of his bed with his shoes on trying to haul Specimen onto the floor.

"He's not hurting your dumb bed, Joe!" John Jr. raised his booming baritone to top Joe's adolescent squeak.

"What's going on here!" I roared.

Faces reddened by anger, they stood glaring at each other.

"Well?" I placed my hands on my hips drill-sergeant-style.

"Specimen sleeps in my bed and stinks it up." Joe presented his side with a flare.

"Joe is going to tell Babs about Laura," responded J.J., flashing angry blue eyes at his younger brother.

"Fighting won't settle the problem, boys." I arranged my voice to soothing calm. "What we need here is communication— a two-way dialogue." I glanced from one mad face to the other. "Communication is the key."

Four eyes dropped, Joe stepped off the bed, and J.J. put down the chair he'd raised in self-defense.

" 'And be kind to one another, tenderhearted, forgiving each other, just as . . . ' "

" ' . . . God in Christ also has forgiven you,' "[29] said my eldest.

"Good! You remember the verse! Now it just doesn't do any good at all to *say* these things and not *do* them; now does it?" I shifted my gaze from one son to the other and waited for them to cool down.

"Maybe you can compromise."

Joe and J.J. sat down on their beds and waited for Mother's wisdom. "J.J., you know that Specimen is really an outside dog, don't you? And Joe, you realize that you shouldn't interfere with your brother's girlfriends . . ."

They nodded affirmatively.

"So?" I prodded them along to a natural conclusion.

"Sorry, Joe," offered my eldest. "I'll give Specimen a bath. Then if he hops into your bed, at least he'll be clean."

Joe's face lighted up. "Thanks, J.J.! And I would never tell Babs about Laura! I just said that because I was mad."

"Now shake hands," I suggested.

"Forget it, Mom," they chorused. "We're not babies anymore!"

"Can't win 'em all," I advised myself.

"Hey, Mom, I smell smoke!" Joe leaped off his bed and ran for the living room. "Mom!" The sound of his scream lifted me off my feet.

When I reached Joe, he held up his cupped hands out to me. "Mom," he said softly, "Buddy is dead."

Tears filled my eyes at the sight of Joe's pet lying lifeless in his hands.

"It's smoke inhalation, Mom. We learned about it in biology," offered John Jr.

Hugging Joe and his dead parakeet, I smoothed his hair away from his hot forehead the way I had when he was a little boy crying.

J.J. came and sat next to him, saying nothing.

Jumping up, I closed the living room window as hatred rose in my soul. When I looked outside, I could see Mrs. O had moved the smokestack.

"It's aimed right at our living room!" I exclaimed. Without a backward glance, I raced down the basement stairs.

"Where are you going, Mom?" J.J. followed after me.

"To water our lawn, J.J.—right next to their smokestack."

Pent-up fury moved me at lightning speed as I stormed out the basement door. "This means *war!*"

9 / Grad

"Barak said to her, 'If you go with me, I will go; but if you don't go with me, I won't go.' "[30]

"Good morning, Martha!" The middle-aged man in *my* office sitting behind *my* desk with *my* telephone receiver in his hand addressed me confidently.

"Who are you?" I replied uneasily to weasel-eyes underneath medium brown hair.

Ignoring my question, he waved a thin hand toward one of my office chairs and said, "Sit down, please."

I sat.

"Martha," he began, fingering one of my pens, "Mr. Kleaver thinks you need some help around the store." Lifting his beady orbs and studying me carefully, he continued. "Since your accident—I understand you received severe a whiplash—you will not be feeling quite up to par; therefore, I've been hired to assist you." He leaned back comfortably in my chair and twined his thin fingers behind his narrow head.

"Who are you?" I repeated my previous question.

"Len," he replied simply.

For some reason unknown to me, shivers shilly-shallied up and down my spine as though the very name Len would spell disaster for me at work. "Mr. Kleaver didn't tell me . . ."

"When he and I discussed it, I felt it wouldn't be necessary until you were back to work, and here you are!" He smiled over teeth too small to be human.

Instant dislike of this rat-like man permeated my system. "Oh." Trying not to twist my fingers, I looked down at my hands and folded them tightly together.

"Now"—he leaned forward in my desk chair—"I understand you have had some financial problems."

My right hand began to twitch.

"Martha? Did you hear me?" His beady eyes demanded my attention.

"It depends on what you mean," I responded softly.

"Is there something wrong with your voice?" His tone reduced my self-esteem to that of a snail.

I cleared my throat. "Just a frog, I guess."

The frown lines in his forehead appeared to be chiseled from stone, and his thin lips barely covered his tiny teeth. "It seems you've run up some massive bills here, Martha. Kleav wants me to straighten this out and get us on target again."

"Kleav?" In spite of my best efforts, my hands wrung their fingers and fiddled with my wedding ring.

"I see you've done some major renovating . . ."

My stomach twisted into a nauseous knot. I could see the handwriting on the wall spelling, "M A R T H A—FIRED!"

Len quickly shuffled through the stack of bills. "Well?"

Tears shot to my eyes. Embarrassed beyond my endurance, I blurted out, "Well, then just say it! I'm fired! You've been given the authority to give me the ax, so just do it then!" Unable to sit there, I jumped up from my chair and tried to run for the door.

"Martha! Wait!" For a moment Len's voice sounded sincere.

Stopping by the door, I waited.

"Martha, come back and sit down. Nothing could be further from the truth . . ."

Angrily wiping the tears from my cheeks, I tried to compose myself. Again I sat down.

While Len continued to drone on about the bills, the business, and the problems he could foresee, a verse bombed around in my head.

As soon as the inquisition finished, I ran from the room to

the freshly decorated staff lounge and dug a Bible out from the drawer where I kept a few for Fred and others who might need some inspiration at a moment's notice. "Good thing for me I did this," I muttered, thumbing through the pages. "Ah, here it is, 'The words of his mouth were smoother than butter, but war was in his heart; his words were softer than oil, yet were they drawn swords.' "[31]

"I know Len is no good. I don't trust him for a minute. I don't care what he says."

Just then, my eyes fell upon the verse that followed what I'd just read. "Cast thy burden upon the Lord, and he shall sustain thee; he shall never suffer the righteous to be moved."[32]

Sitting back on the deep purple velveteen-covered brass chair I'd ordered for the room, I felt calm approach me. "Yes," I said aloud, "that is excellent advice for Fred. I'll be sure to tell him that next time he has a crisis." The quiet vanished as softly as it had arrived.

Nerves ajar, I returned to work. "Somehow I'll get through the day," I comforted myself, "and then I'll think about this tonight—when I have more time."

Drulene took over the cash register from me at 4:00 o'clock. "How's it going, Martha? Don't you just *love* Len?"

Not wanting to lie, I answered, "I'm in a hurry, Drulene. Our parakeet, Buddy, died a few days ago, and I need to get home on time for a change."

"What's that got to do with anything?" she whined.

Grabbing my cash drawer, I departed. I should have seen the look in her eyes, but I didn't.

Too upset to notice anything other than my pain, I ran for the safety and refuge of home.

Deciding to walk home, I relaxed a bit. "The air smells terrific! Who knows, maybe I won't even get a sinus attack from what-ever blooms in June!"

By the time I reached our driveway, my nose informed me of ill winds blowing from Mrs. O's backyard.

"Oh no! I am so sick of the reek!" Storming up the drive, I passed right by our back door and headed for the fence. "Hello! Anybody home?" I yelled.

No response.

"That does it! I've just about had enough!" I groused as I grabbed our green garden hose and attached the large water sprinkler to the end. "I guess she just didn't notice the last time I watered our lawn next to their smokestack! And I know for certain she didn't know that her smoke killed our baby bird!" I hurried back to the outside tap and turned it on. "There! That should do it!" In satisfaction I watched as my own personal rainstorm moved up and over their smokestack. I viewed with contempt as the water moved over the smokestack, hovered for a few moments, and then began its downward move toward our lawn again. "There! If that doesn't do it, I'll set it to stop position right over the stack. This will just be a mild warning." Turning on my heel, I waltzed back to our house.

"Hey, Mom! Whatcha doin' watering the edge of our yard?" George's voice drifted down the stairs as I removed my jacket.

"Nothing!" I lied.

He bounded down the stairs to greet me. "Yes, you are. You're watering Mrs. O's smokestack!"

"George, not now." I plodded up the stairs, passing him in the middle.

"Okay. Did you know I'm a 'Latchkey Kid'?"

"What does that mean, George?" Only mildly interested, I proceeded to the kitchen.

"That means nobody's home when I get here, and I could get into trouble! I learned about it in school today—on a video."

"Is that a promise, or a threat, George?" Playfully I cuffed him on the shoulder.

"I'm serious, Mom. With the world we live in today, I shouldn't be left alone."

"Nonsense, George. I trust you," I replied cheerfully.

"Left to my own devices, I could even be in movies . . ."

Alarms went off in my mother's head. "Sit down, George. What have you been learning at school?"

"Just that there are all kinds of terrible people around who try to capture children and drug them and—"

"George, listen to me. You are only here for one hour usually before I arrive home from Kleaver's. And then, you can always call Jean. We've been through all that." Crossing my arms in front of me, I studied him carefully. "Definitely you are showing signs of becoming a teenager, George."

"How can you tell?" His blue eyes gave full concentration anytime we discussed him or his interests.

"Well, for one thing, you've got some peach fuzz growing on the top of your upper lip."

"Aw, Mom." George blushed with manly pride. "It's not peach fuzz. It's dirt!"

"For another, you're coming up with some strange ideas about what you hear at school—"

"So what's for supper?" George interrupted.

"—but the main thing that let's me know you're almost a teen is your appetite!" I handed him an apple from the bowl on the counter.

"This isn't food!" George said and refused to take it. "It's garbage!"

"Are these the sounds of family fun I hear?" J.J.'s voice appeared in the kitchen before his body made it all the way up the stairs.

"Hi, J.J. Why are you so late?" I turned to face my eldest.

"If we had two cars around here, I wouldn't have to beg rides all the time." He grabbed a couple of pieces of bread and stuffed them into his mouth. "I missed the bus."

"Where's Joe?" Pouring two glasses of milk, I placed them on the kitchen counter.

"Dad's giving him a ride," John Jr. responded, gulping the milk in three swallows.

George didn't touch his milk or the apple. "See ya," he said.

"Where are you going?"

"Out on my bike."

"Be home before supper."

"I won't, ha, ha." Grinning broadly, he whisked the glass of milk off the kitchen counter, drank it noisily, and shoved the apple in his pocket.

"Thanks, George," I commented, giving him a hug.

"Sure, Mom," he replied, slapping me on the shoulder. "I aim to please."

As soon as George had clattered down the basement stairs and slammed the outside door, John Jr. announced, "I need money for Grad, Mom—lotsa money."

An uneasy feeling gripped the pit of my stomach. I knew many of the other graduates would be partying all night—some in distant towns. Rumors of car accidents, drinking bouts, drug use, and graduating mothers-to-be struck terror in my soul. "Exactly what are your plans, J.J.?"

He struck an easy stance. "As you know, Mom, Babs and I have been writing for the last couple of months . . ."

I nodded affirmatively. "Continue," I responded, feeling the air charge with tension.

"So, well, Babs, that is, Babs and me, I mean, Babs and *I*, would like to attend the ceremony together. For that, I will need money for the tux, and then there's the class ring, and our Grad sweat shirts with all our signatures printed on the back, the Grad pencils, pens, paper clips . . ."

"*Paper clips?* Grad *paper clips?*" My eyebrows reached my hairline in less than two seconds.

"I don't have to get the paper clips, Mom—even though they *are* gold plated, but there are a few other items everyone is getting."

I decided against tangling with the term "everyone" and moved on to more important issues. "What about the activities?"

"Activities?" His innocent blue eyes sparkled too brightly.

"Yes. You know. The things you do after the ceremony is over."

"Oh! Yeah! That!" He cleared his throat. "Well, there will be some parties, probably a dance, a Bar-B-Que, and a breakfast on Sunday."

Forcing my voice to condition-calm, I said, "Sunday?"

"Uh, yeah!" His voice squeaked as though fourteen again.

My dander rose dangerously. "John Jr., the graduation ceremony is Friday night. Are you trying to tell me the partying will be going on from Friday night to Sunday morning?"

"Actually, Mom, Sunday afternoon are the bed races—"

"Bed races?" The hair on my arms stood up. "What do you mean, bed races?"

"Oh, it's great, Mom—kind of like go-carts or small cars! See, they strip down beds—any kind, put wheels on them and different teams race." Carefully he continued. "See, four guys—one at each corner of the bed—run down a road with a girl in the bed. Whoever gets there first wins, but nobody wants Sharon because she weighs over two hundred pounds. Babs is kinda light, so . . ."

"Forget the bed races, J.J. I won't hear of it." Snatching the kettle off the stove, I filled it with cold water and put it back on a burner to heat.

"What's wrong with bed races?" J.J.'s blue eyes snapped with anger.

"I said *no*. That's what's wrong with bed races," I retorted.

"Then I suppose you're not going to let me go to anything else either!"

"I didn't say that."

The kettle whistled its piercing shriek from the stove.

Flipping up the lid, I slammed a tea bag into a cup and poured boiling water over it. Then I wrung out the bag with its paper-labeled string on the back of a spoon.

Meanwhile, J.J. glared at the ceiling.

"J.J.," I began softly while spooning sugar into my tea, "this may be difficult time for both of us . . ."

"That's easy for *you* to say! Nobody's ruining your graduation!"

"That's not true, J.J. My mother ruined mine years ago." Stirring my tea, I smiled, trying to lighten the situation.

"Just because Gran ruined your Grad doesn't mean you have to destroy mine!" With that he stormed out of the kitchen.

Standing alone, I felt totally abandoned. I heard his books crash to the floor, his closet doors being flung open, and his desk chair thump against something solid. "Why does it have to be so hard, Lord? It's not my fault people live the way they do. I can't condone an entire weekend of celebrating!"

"Martha! We're home!" John's voice arrived right on time.

"Hooray, the cavalry!" I shouted down the stairs.

Moments later, John and I sat side by side on the living room sofa. "So what's the problem, Martha?"

"John, we need a second car."

"Oh, is that all?" He gave me quick hug while reaching for his steaming tea.

"No, that is not all, John," I shot back. "This is important! For one thing, I could certainly use one. I get tired of walking home from work, or having to wait until you pick me up somewhere."

"But you're lucky, Martha. You can shop right on the job!" His twinkling blue eyes told me he was teasing.

"John, please be serious." I sipped my tea and waited for his mood to change.

"Okay. I'm ready. Give it your best shot." He sat back and turned on his full attention.

"I think it would help John Jr.—give him more responsibility—if he could also drive a car that would be more like his own. After all, graduation is coming up, and he's hoping to take Babs, and . . ."

" . . . and you're hoping to bribe him with a car." John took a swig of tea.

"Well, I wouldn't want to use that term, but I do think it might help him to make some right decisions about the after-grad activities."

"What do they want to do—stay out all night?" John zeroed right in on target.

"For the whole weekend, John."

John leaned forward, placing his cup on the coffee table. "Where is J.J. now?"

"In his room sulking."

"I'll go have a talk with him."

"What about a second car?"

John didn't look back. He talked as he walked out of the living room. "You've needed a car for a long time, Martha. Now seems to be as good a time as any to do something about it."

Whispering a small prayer of gratitude, I hunted around the house for Joe. "Joe?" I called down the basement stairs.

"Here, Mom," he answered from the recesses of the floor below me.

Descending the stairs, I located him at one end of the basement. "What are you doing down here, Joe?"

"Thinking," he replied, sitting on what was left of an old chair. "Pull up the floor and sit down, Mom."

"What?"

"Nothing, Mom. Here." Moving off the chair seat, he dusted it off with his hands.

"I've been thinking about Buddy, Joe." Carefully I perched on the edge of the piece of chair.

"Me too."

Tears stung my eyes as I watched my fifteen-year-old almost-man bite his lower lip to stop the trembling. "What about another parakeet?"

"No. I don't think so."

"How 'bout a guinea pig—to keep Ben company?"

"No. Pigs are for George, not me."

"What's for you, Joe?" Gently I probed and hoped he wouldn't shut me out.

His stocky frame seemed smaller as he replied, "I don't know."

"Well, then, let's find out—together, big guy." I mussed his carefully combed hair.

"Hey, Mom, don't touch the merchandise." He winced as though I'd touched him with a live coal.

"So, what about a turtle, Joe?"

Joe's deep brown eyes rolled around and he squinted his eyelids.

"Well?" I folded my hands together and waited.

"What kind of turtle?"

"I don't know *what kind*, Joe," I chuckled good-naturedly; "any kind you want."

Straightening his back he leaped to his feet. "A snapping turtle!"

"Don't be ridiculous. Why a snapping turtle?"

"I can take him to wrestling matches as my mascot!"

"I see," I responded straight-faced.

"When can we go?"

"In the next day or two. Your father's going to take me out to buy a car. Maybe we can look at the same time."

Joe's face lit up like a lighthouse. "A *car*? You mean it, Mom? A car?" He danced around in circles. "A car. I can't believe it! A car!" Suddenly he stopped dead and faced me. "Mom," he demanded, grabbing my shoulders, "does J.J. know?"

"Probably. Your dad is talking to him about it right now." Joe rubbed his chin thoughtfully. "Is he going to get to drive it?"

"I suppose so. Why?"

Like a horse trader in triumph, my middle son announced, "Then *I* get to fix it!"

"We can talk about it later, Joe. I'm going to fix supper."

"Hey, Mom?"

"What, Joe?" I stopped on the middle of the stairs.

"I turned the water sprinkler off for you. I think George moved it too close to the O's yard. It looked kind of funny, though. The sprinkler must have stuck or something because all that was coming out of their smokestack was little wisps, and the water washed it right away."

"Oh," I replied, heading guiltily up the stairs . . .

Over the next couple of days, my diet, exercise, and car search kept me occupied. Managing to finally see five pounds less on the scale after three days' starving, I didn't care that my temper thinned as well.

When my eldest approached me with his graduation dilemma, a preoccupied mother sat at the kitchen table counting calories.

"Mom, you're not going to believe this!" J.J. threw his book on the floor beside the table and paced around the room like a caged gorilla.

"What happened, J.J.?" My eyes glued themselves to the calorie counter, while my fingers steadily tapped the buttons on my new calculator.

"I'm not going to graduation."

"Of course you are, dear, and Andrea Gray won't believe her eyes when I show up paper thin!"

"You know when I told you Babs would be moving back?"

"Yes, I remember," I replied, still adding and subtracting.

"Well, her dad can't get away yet—maybe not for six months!"

"Ask Laura then."

"Mom, how could I?" He flopped down in a chair across from me, shoving the table six inches to the left.

"John! I am trying to count here!"

"Mom! I am trying to graduate here!" His blue eyes bored holes into my irritated hazel ones.

Reorganizing myself, I suggested. "Okay, dear. Here's how it's done. Just call up Laura and ask her."

"What if she says she won't go?"

"You're not going to know that until you try, are you?"

He stretched out his long legs and accidentally kicked my right shin.

"Ow!" I stood up. "John Jr., how many times have I told you . . ."

" . . . not to stick my legs out." He pulled them back, mildly resembling a limp French fry, as his body formed an S-shape, which began at the table, continued on his chair, and wound up where his feet met the floor.

"Did you and Dad pick out a car yet?" Suddenly his expression transformed itself from a sulky pout to silky smooth.

"As a matter of fact, J.J., we may close a deal later this evening—after supper."

"Wow, Mom!"

"Maybe you'd like to take Laura to graduation in my new car . . ."

"Good idea! I'll go phone her right now!" He moved across the room in one giant leap. "By the way, Mom, how's your leg—where I kicked it?"

"Fine, honey. Go and make your call."

By nine o'clock that evening, I sat behind the wheel of my new-to-me automobile. Proud husband John made mock signs of terror as I drove us around the block a few times.

"Oh, John, I just love it!" Steering carefully, I floored the accelerator, passing a few parked cars in a blur.

"Martha, you just ran a stop sign!"

"Did I?" I giggled. "Just too excited, I guess."

Crouching down in the passenger seat, John put his right hand over his eyes. "Guess I'll just pray."

"Nonsense, my dear. It will be just fine. You'll see."

"But will the other drivers of the world survive?" He cracked a grin under the cover of his left arm.

"Better watch it, John, I'm driving!"

"Pull over to a parking spot for a minute, will you?" His voice sounded serious.

"Sure, honey, what's the matter?" Quickly I found a place and pulled the car over.

"Martha, I've been meaning to talk to you about Andrea." My husband took a deep breath, waiting for my reaction.

Staring straight ahead, I kept my hands on the wheel and my eyes on the car parked ahead of me.

"Andrea feels hurt by your lack of friendship, Martha."

"Well, John, I have something to discuss with you too," I blurted.

"Go ahead, Martha." John tipped his seat back and crossed his arms in front of him.

"It's about the neighbors next door. I am sick and tired of that horrible smoke chugging right into our living room, and it killed Buddy."

"Martha, parakeets die. We don't always know the reasons. Don't you think that accusation is a little heavy?"

"No, I don't, John. You used to be the mayor of our fair city. I want you to sue them." I crossed my arms and leaned them on the horn.

"Martha!" John shouted above the horn. "Get your arms off the horn!"

"Excuse me!" I snapped. "At least it works. What are you going to do about the neighbors' smoke?"

"Nothing, Martha. They are allowed to live in quiet enjoyment. That's the law."

Shock forced my mouth open. "Nothing? Well, I'm going to do *something*!"

My husband shook his head from side to side. "All right, Martha, it's up to you." He touched my right shoulder gently. "Andrea has been voted Woman of the Year because of her successful Carts for the Underprivileged Poor project. The school board has invited her to give the roll call at John Jr.'s graduation."

Stunned, I couldn't answer. Instead, I turned the key in the ignition. Flipping on the left-hand turn signal, I waited to pull back into traffic.

"One more thing, Martha." John's words cut me like a hot knife through soft butter. "I've accepted the invitation from the graduation committee to be the main speaker."

Pain, rejection, and loneliness seared through me.

By the next day, after I'd picked up my compact car, I listened to J.J.'s tirade about how Laura wouldn't go to graduation with him because George told Laura about Babs. "My own brother! An informer! If Babs won't go with me, I won't go!"

"J.J.," I replied, "I'm certain we can work out something."

"When? Grad is in two weeks!" Anger flushed his cheeks red.

My shoulders sagged. "Son, things have a way of working out. Why don't you take my car for a trial run?"

"Sure, Mom," he responded sadly, "but it won't help." He did, however, take the keys, start the car, and depart down our driveway in less than three minutes.

I stood at the living room window alone. "My son is facing one of the most important days of his life—his high school graduation—and Andrea Gray, who has no children of her own, will award my son his diploma." I watched as the smokestack next door began to chug, sending its foul, dark wind my way. Refusing defeat, I straightened my spine as hope shed a ray of light.

"Deborah!"

10 / Gran

" . . . O my soul, march on with strength."[33]

I stood at the kitchen counter, watering the telephone receiver with my tears. "Oh, Mom, J.J. refuses to attend his own graduation, John has a very close woman-friend, Andrea Gray, and I'm still ten pounds overweight." I sniffed and wiped my nose with a flowered facial tissue.

"He *must* go to his own graduation, Martha. Stop crying. I have an idea. Leave it with your mother, dear."

"What idea?" Curiosity dried my tears.

"Now, go and fix your face. I'll phone you back in a little while."

While waiting for the telephone to ring, I picked up my well-read Bible and headed for the sofa in the living room. "Psalms are always good in a crisis," I comforted myself, sitting down, flipping pages.

"Give thanks to the Lord, for he is good; his love endures forever. Let Israel say: 'His love endures forever.' Let the house of Aaron say: 'His love endures forever.' Let those who fear the Lord say: 'His love endures forever.' In my anguish I cried to the Lord, and he answered by setting me free. . . .The Lord is with me; he is my helper. I will look in triumph on my enemies. . . .It is better to take refuge in the Lord than to trust in princes."[34]

A soothing balm swept over my soul. "Why don't I realize God loves me? I say it, but I don't really believe it in my heart.

If I did, I wouldn't worry about all this—maybe—"

The telephone sounded like church chimes pealing, "Hello, hello. Here's help, here's help."

Jumping to my feet, I raced to answer it. "Mom?"

"Yes, dear. Don't act so surprised. I told you I'd phone you back."

The sound of my mother's voice lifted my spirits. "You've always been there for me, Mom. You and Dad taught me how to pray when I still liked to swing on Daddy's necktie. Life was so simple then . . ." I could feel tears filling my eyes.

"Nonsense, Martha."

"What?"

"Life is never easy—wasn't then; isn't now."

"But, Mom, you were always so strong! Even when Daddy died five years ago, you seemed so solid. I can still remember you calling yourself Napoleon when I was little because you were only five feet tall."

Mother joined me in wandering down memory lane for a moment. "That's because you were so full of energy—climbing trees, putting fire crackers in the neighbors' begonias, and hiding from your Sunday-school teachers."

"I'll always remember coming home to the smell of freshly baked bread and homemade cookies. How did you stay so slim eating food like that?"

"Wasn't so slim, Martha. Styles have changed, that's all."

"Oh, Mom!" I exclaimed, my voice choking with emotion, "it's going to be so good to have you here for John Jr.'s graduation. You're just the medicine I need!"

"I won't be coming, Martha."

"Not you too!"

"But Babs will." Mom chuckled into the phone. "Let me explain. I've already contacted the airlines and made the necessary arrangements for Babs to be able to use my ticket if it's okay with her parents."

"But how . . ."

"Martha, when will you ever learn to trust me? Never mind *how*. All you have to do is tell that grandson of mine he will be attending graduation with the girl of his choice."

"Oh, Mom, thank you, but I will miss your being there."

"Can't be helped. The deed is done. Tell J.J. to give me a call, and I'll fill him in on the details."

"You're still Napoleon—even at age sixty-two!"

"Have a good time, dear, and I'll be praying about your other-woman problems."

"Mother, I didn't say—"

"Didn't have to. Tell J.J. to call me."

After hanging up the receiver a mixture of shame and anticipation caused my stomach to rock around. "I feel so silly that she could see right through me about Andrea. Now at least John Jr. will have a good Grad." My stomach churned another turn. "But what about me?"

Over the next few days, I starved myself into a dress one size too small. "Not bad, if I do say so myself," I said to my image in the full-length hall mirror.

Events mounted from a swirl to a whirlwind by graduation night.

Babs arrived safely and stayed with friends, and John Jr. managed to escort his ladylove with a flair.

During the ceremony, tall, thin Andrea Gray received honors for her most recent achievements among the young people in John Jr.'s high school.

My husband John delivered an excellent speech.

Andrea Gray awarded my eldest son his graduation diploma.

J.J. received the award for Outstanding Male Student.

Joe cheered.

George squirmed.

And I lived with nausea and stomach cramps.

By the end of that week, my stomach problems caused me enough distress to see a doctor.

"What seems to be the problem, Martha?"

"I don't know. My stomach seems upset all the time."

"Been feeling that way long?"

"For a few months, I guess."

"Hmm," he replied, busily writing on a pad of paper.

"What do you think it is?"

"Don't know, Martha." He ripped the paper off the pad and

handed it to me. "Here. Take it as directed. In the meantime, I'd like to order a few tests."

"Oh," I replied quickly, "I don't have time for tests right now. You see, my son has just graduated, and I'm in over my head at work, and . . ."

The next morning, I found myself at the hospital drinking disgusting chalky fluids after having starved all night.

"At least this will be good for my dieting," I said, trying to console myself.

By the end of the week, I sat waiting in the physician's office, nervously twisting my wedding ring.

"Martha Christian?"

"Yes!" Jumping to my feet, I followed the stern-looking nurse to the doctor's inner sanctum.

After a few nervous moments of waiting, the medical man appeared. "How are you feeling today, Martha?" His eyes scanned the pages of my file folder lying neatly on his desk.

"Is it serious?" I whispered through a dry, cracked throat.

The learned physician took off his half-glasses, laid them on his desk, and folded his hands.

"It's serious," I suggested.

"How do you *feel*?" The M.D. perched on the edge of his desk—one foot on the floor, the other dangling.

"You look a little like the bald eagle I saw at the mall yesterday," I commented cheerily.

"What?" His bushy eyebrows raised.

"I feel better today." My stomach jabbed me for lying.

Sliding off the desk corner, he wended his way around the room until he deposited himself heavily in his cushioned armchair.

"How do *you* feel?" I questioned sincerely. "You look terribly tired."

He positioned his half-glasses on his nose and glanced over them at the papers lying before him on his desk. "Martha, what we have here"—he waved his hands like a benediction—"could be called a *successful woman's syndrome*."

"Oh my! Is it serious?" My attention span increased one hundredfold.

"We often find this condition in Type A women. It doesn't matter whether she is a homemaker or a corporate executive." He carefully placed his spectacles on top of my file folder.

"Type *A*." I frowned. "Is that something to do with my blood type?"

"No," he responded. "You could call it irritable bowel syndrome. It can cause stabbing, burning pains that resemble an ulcer."

"Is it an ulcer?" Fear rocketed through me.

"No."

"Oh." Breathing a sigh of relief, I dutifully waited for him to continue.

"Symptoms of this malady can be nausea, indigestion, pain, and so forth accompanied by intestinal spasms—"

"What can I call it?" I blurted into his discourse.

"What?" Surprise at my bold behavior forced his placid forehead to crease into a frown.

"What *is* it?" I leaned forward in my chair to take charge of the situation just as I'd learned from Ginny's notes on being assertive. "What can I *call* it?"

Irritation formed along his upper lip, causing it to purse. "You could call it a stomachache." He clipped his words.

"Is that what it is?"

"Martha, please give me a moment to explain it, will you?"

"Sorry." Chastised, I crumpled into my chair.

"Maybe nothing is wrong. We'll have to wait and see."

"Then what shall I do?"

"I'll give you a prescription for the pain. Come back and see me in a week."

Duly dismissed, my guilt carried me home. "What's wrong with me? Why can't he find anything?" Questions roared around my head as I sped down the street and went whizzing through a stop sign.

The scream of a siren glued my eyes to my rearview mirror. "Must be a fire," I mumbled, trying to find a way to move over to the side.

Flashing lights caught my attention next. I floored the gas

pedal to get to the right lane and muttered, "That should give them plenty of room."

As my speed increased, the siren behind me screamed louder, and my heartbeat escalated from thump-thump to thumpity-thump-thump. *I* was the reason for the siren! I heard an amplified voice saying, "Move over, lady!"

Frantic, I pulled the car to the side of the road and stopped. My insides caved in as I looked in my rearview mirror. Watching the uniformed policeman casually turn off his loud, irritating warning device added anger to my fear. When he left me sitting in my car while he gathered his clipboard, adjusted his mirror sunglasses, and dusted off his shiny shoes, fury rose in my chest like a hungry dinosaur checking out dinner-on-the-foot.

He sauntered over to my car. "Going pretty fast there, lady."

"I wasn't until you started chasing me," I snapped.

"Let's see your driver's license," he responded.

"Certainly," I said with a calm born of resentment. I began digging through my purse. "Let's see, I know it's in here . . ."

The mirrored eyes above a cruel mouth seemed to say, "Hurry up. I don't have all day."

Perspiration beaded on my forehead. "That's funny," I remarked, "it was here yesterday. I wonder if I used my other purse . . ."

The long arm of the law shifted his gun belt and assumed a forceful stance.

"I've just come from the doctor's office," I commented, shuffling through the glove compartment of my new car. "Ah! Here are my insurance papers. Would you like to see those?"

"Just your license, lady—if you have one," he replied without humor.

"Of course I have one," I shot back. "I just can't seem to find it at this precise moment!" Pain throttled through my stomach. "I'll just check my purse again." I scrambled through it one more time. "Here it is!" Triumphantly I handed over my right to drive.

The unkind officer of the law accepted my bit of plastic, handed it back, and announced, "Okay, lady, you ran a stop sign and exceeded the speed limit by forty miles per hour." With a pencil stub from behind his left ear, he began to write on his clipboard.

My goose is cooked, I thought, watching him prepare my fate. *What would Ginny say about being assertive?* I stared at the pencil moving on the paper. "Just a minute!"

Mildly surprised, he looked up.

"Uh, I didn't know you were chasing *me*, and I was trying to get out of your way! If I'd known you were after me, I would have stopped immediately! In fact, if you noticed, sir, I did try to pull over, but there was no place to go!" I burst into tears.

"Are you all right?" For the first time *human* connected with the being who held my immediate future in his hands.

"No, I'm not," I sobbed. "My husband has lost interest in me, and my oldest son is leaving home, and now the doctor says I have a syndrome!" Real tears (propelled by the anguish of being caught) coursed down my cheeks.

"It can't be that bad, can it?" the officer said, looking uncomfortable at the sight of a woman crying.

"It's worse!" Wiping my eyes, I leaned confidently toward this stranger who I hoped would understand where no one else had.

He took a quick step back and the stub of a pencil was returned to its home behind the state patrol's ear. "Listen, ma'am, I'm sorry I scared you like that—chasing you and all. You understand—I have to do my job."

"Oh, of course!" I carefully placed my driver's license in my wallet and shoved it into my purse. "I'm a working person too."

"Okay, now you drive carefully—you hear?"

"Yes, sir!" I saluted, then started the engine. "Bye!"

One week later, I sat in the doctor's office doubled over with stomach cramps. Fear raised its ugly head as I imagined the worst. By the time I got in to see him, I said, "Is it the big C?"

"Martha," a stand-in doctor replied, "I think you need a rest."

"I am rather tired," I agreed.

"No, I mean, more like a vacation. Why not take a week or so off work and visit somebody?"

"Am I losing my grip? What's wrong with me, Doctor?"

"Maybe nothing—maybe it's stress." The female physician, barely twenty-five years old, searched my eyes for telltale signs of anything I'd care to reveal.

I didn't care to reveal anything. A perfect stranger like the kind officer, yes. A white coat, no. "Hmm," I answered.

"Why not think about it? In the meantime, I'd suggest adding cereal grains, fruits, vegetables, and other bulky items to your diet. Sometimes a diet high in fiber will relieve the symptoms."

And I was dismissed.

When I arrived home after a hard day's work at Kleaver's, and a difficult time at the friendly physician's, I could hear a chorus of angry voices as I wearily climbed the basement stairs.

"Listen, J.J., either *I* get to fix the car, or—"

"*You* listen, Joe! Mom said she'd get you a turtle! Now get outta my life!"

"Yeah! Well, you hog the car all the time!" My middle son replied. Joe's voice screeched so loud the O's must have heard him in their living room. "Anyway, who wants a dumb turtle!"

"You do, Joe! You said so!" J.J.'s rebuttal paled by comparison, although the volume may have exceeded Joe's declaration.

Too weary to get involved in the quarrel, I decided to wait on the stairs and hope they came to an agreement.

"Yeah! Well, I'm going to tell Mom how you raced the school bus and nearly got us all killed when you drove to school last week!"

What? My ears strained for more information.

"You do, and *I'll* tell Mom how you . . ." J.J.'s voice dropped to a level I couldn't hear.

Sounds of scuffling brought me quickly up the stairs and to their room.

When I reached their doorway, I saw Joe holding a chair above him, which was aimed directly for John Jr.'s head.

"Stop it! Stop it! Stop it!" I yelled. "Joe, put down that chair! J.J., go to your room!"

"I'm *in* my room," he retorted saucily.

"Don't you *ever* use that tone with me John Jr.! I disciplined you when you were a child, and I'm perfectly willing to do it again, so hand over your car keys!"

"Aw, Mom . . ." J.J. shoved his hands in his pockets. "I didn't do anything."

"The very idea! Racing a school bus! Why, I never!" Sticking out my right hand, palm up, I waited for the keys.

"Hi, everybody! What's happening?" George bounded into the room and flopped down on Joe's bed—guaranteed to start a war.

"Get off, jerk!" Joe stepped menacingly toward his younger brother.

Undaunted, George looked at me and said, "Do I have to, Mom?"

Shifting my glare from oldest son to middle son, I replied, "It's his bed, George. We have to learn to respect other people's property."

"Joe didn't buy the bed; you did," George pronounced.

"So?" Joe challenged.

"So, nothin'!" George slowly slithered toward the edge of the bed while watching Joe seethe with irritation.

"George, get off," I interjected.

"Say, please." George flashed a grin my direction, bouncing one more time before he leaped to his feet.

I let that one pass.

"Hey, Mom? Can I drive the car in the driveway?" asked George.

George's elder brothers' sighs of relief informed me that I was outnumbered for this round.

"No, George, you may not," I responded, leaving the room.

"All the other kids drive their cars in the driveway," he whined.

"No. I said no." Rubbing my forehead, I tried to remember where I was going as I left John Jr. and Joe's bedroom.

"Mom, you want the *keys*?" John Jr. hollered down the hall after me and my trailing youngest duckling.

"I know where I'm going," I muttered to myself. Turning around, running into George, I shouted, "Forget it! I'm leaving town for a couple of weeks!"

"So, Mom, can I drive your car in the backyard?" George spoke.

A smile spread my lips where they hadn't been for months—genuine relaxation. "George, dear, did you hear me? I'm leaving town, and *no* you may not even *touch* the car except for the outside handles and the inside seats until I return. That is an order from headquarters. Do you understand?"

"You okay, Mom? Maybe I should get you a cold cloth or something. Your eyes look funny." George wrinkled his nose to shove up his glasses.

"On the contrair, my dear, I'm sane for the first time in weeks!" I gave him a quick hug.

"Mom, the word is con-tra-ry. Never mind about the car." My baby's blue eyes flashed friendliness.

"George, tell you what, you go build Ben a space station, and I'm going to wait for your father to come home."

"Am I in trouble?" His eyebrows drew close together.

"No, honey." I smoothed his tousled head. "I'll tell you all about it as soon as I discuss this with your dad. Okay?"

George scrutinized my face for a moment, messed up the hair I'd just straightened, and seriously questioned, "Can I tell the other guys?"

"Certainly, dear. I'm going to make a pot of coffee for your dad's arrival."

"With caffeine?"

"Why?"

"If you make coffee like Dad likes it, this must be *big*!"

An hour later, I sat across the kitchen table from John. "More coffee?"

"Thanks, no, I've had two cups." He took my hand. "When do you want to go?"

"As soon as possible, I think. The doctor seems to feel a change will restore me from the accident, and help my stomach problems as well. Besides, it will be good to see Mom, and she can't afford to come here right now. Oregon is lovely this time of year."

"Have you talked this over with your mother?"

"No. Thought I'd ask you first."

"Thanks." John let go of my hand, leaned back in his chair, and grinned. "Well, let's get packing!"

"Let's?" My eyebrows met my hairline.

"Figure of speech, my dear. I'll make the plane reservations, and you pack. How's that?" He picked up his cup and carried it to the kitchen. "Guess I'd better practice if the kids and I are going to be baching. Have you told Mr. Kleaver?"

"Not yet, but it should be fine. Len is there, and Mr. Kleaver is getting stronger."

A few days later, my plane touched down along the Oregon coast, and in no time I regained my place as Martha, the daughter.

"Oh, Mom, it's good to be home!" Looking around my old room where I'd grown up, the years and the stress melted away.

"Sometimes we can lose our way, Martha. It doesn't matter how young or how old we are. Do you know what I mean?"

I took in the essence of my mother in a glance—barely five feet tall, snow-white hair pulled tightly into a bun, she gave the appearance of fragility. Her exterior, however, housed a backbone made of pure steel. Mother's wisdom developed from her prayer life and her complete dependence upon God in every circumstance. During my formative years, her presence in our home permeated the house with quiet strength. Mother challenged her daily tasks. Her vitality and energy sparked Dad during his long illness. Her great love comforted his passing from this life to the next. "Yes, Mom, I know exactly what you mean, and I've got a friend to show me the way."

"A friend? Is someone else coming along later?"

"No." I laughed easily. "She's already here, Mom. Her name's Deborah." I picked up my Bible from my unpacked suitcase and held it close to me.

"Ah," she replied, "I understand." And she left me alone with God, my thoughts, and Deborah.

As the days passed, Deborah's song became my melody. "Martha's tune. I like that." I spoke to a snail, poking its head out of its seashell.

Sitting by myself on a blanket on the fine sands of a windswept beach in Oregon, the roar of the gray-blue waves placed music in my soul. "I'm seeing the awesome power of God with my own eyes—what men and women of ages past have seen."

Taking a small Bible from my jacket pocket, I opened it and read.

"Deborah . . . sang this song: 'When the princes in Israel take the lead, when the people willingly offer themselves—praise the Lord!' "[35]

Taking a small notebook and pen from my other jacket pocket, I wrote: (1) I must be *willing*. Some shackles shifted loose from my soul, and I read on.

"Listen . . . I will sing to the Lord. . . . I will make music to the Lord, the God of Israel."[36]

Next point I wrote: (2) I will sing praise to God *every day* no matter what happens—and try to mean it. I'd heard anything practiced for thirty days would become habit. Hope replaced a chain around my heart.

Continuing on, I read the Bible, then wrote my understanding of what I'd read.

By the end of the day, I reviewed the rest of my list:

(3) As the mountains quaked before God's power in Deborah's time, the world today trembles on the brink of disaster; therefore, I will remember God's sovereignty.

(4) Things were really rough until Deborah, Rebekah's nurse, became a mother in Israel.

a. *Mother* means giving birth (usually with pain), bearing life, inspiring others, and giving comfort.

b. As a mother, I am *precious* to God.

(5) When a mother battles in the will of God, even the heavens cooperate. For example, a cloudburst contributed to the victory in the war against Sisera.

(6) Deborah did not shrink from the call of duty—even though it meant going to war alongside Barak.

(7) Deborah obeyed God.[37]

Closing my eyes, I felt the presence of the Comforter: "O my soul, march on with strength."[38]

Opening my eyes, the world appeared fresh. The thundering waves swept through my system as I picked up my things and strolled along the edge of the icy water. Alone on the beach, I watched the sky streak pink and shivered as the air turned cold. "Lord," I whispered, "I know it's time to go."

Home.

11 / Wimple

"Sisera gathered together his nine hundred iron chariots and all the men with him, from Harosheth Haggoyim to the Kishon River."[39]

"I'm healed, John! I haven't had a stomach pain in three days." I bounced alongside my husband in the airport terminal.

"That's great, Martha. Now, where are your baggage checks?"

"In my purse. Let's find a table." I glanced around for a corner, or flat surface. "There's one!"

"Martha, once upon a time in a land far away, I knew a woman who didn't have to empty her purse every time she needed to find something." Once again my spouse waited while I hunted through, dropped, and finally dumped my wallet, keys, combs, lipsticks, paper clips, pens, pencils, crayons, and other odds and ends onto the already-cluttered table.

"Oh, John. Don't grumble." I squeezed his arm and pulled him close. "I feel better than I have in weeks." Still pawing through my purse, I zipped up all the compartments but one. Then I dumped the contents of the remaining pocket out on a wide cement railing. Out popped the baggage checks. "See?" I waved them under his nose. "No problem!" Gathering my gear, I popped it all back into my purse.

Taking my arm, he guided me toward the baggage department. "Martha, there's something I want to discuss with you."

A sense of foreboding gripped the pit of my stomach. Trying

145

to ignore it, I fixed my countenance to appear calm and replied as casually as terror would allow. "Oh?"

Handing the tickets to the baggage clerk, John turned toward me.

I studied his face for clues. "John, did I tell you that Mother may be picking up her water color painting again?" (I thought I read *Andrea Gray* in his eyes.)

His face lighted up momentarily. "I'm glad to hear it, Martha." Then his expression changed as he spoke, "Martha, as I said, there is something I'd like to discuss with you—"

"Oops! Ow!" I lurched to the left. "John, wait. I twisted my ankle."

John, deep in thought, kept walking.

"John!" Whipping off my left shoe, I discovered that the heel was broken. "John, will you *wait*?"

With a big smile gracing his elegant face, my husband had discovered I was missing. Immediately by my side, he chuckled heartily. "I wondered why you didn't answer, Martha."

I grabbed his arm for balance and stood on one foot stork-style. "John," I grumbled, "you've raised your sons to be just like you—thoughtless!" Using his arm for support, I removed my other shoe and stood in my stocking feet. "What am I going to do? If I walk this way, my stockings will be ruined. On the other hand, if I walk with one shoe on and one shoe off, I'll ruin one stocking."

"I could carry you piggyback," joked my husband.

"Great idea, John!" My face beamed at his solution.

John leaped back as though hit by lightning. "Martha, I was *teasing*!"

"Well, you shouldn't say things you don't mean. I learned that from Ginny's—" Realizing I'd said too much, I clamped my mouth shut and hoped he wouldn't notice.

He didn't. He was too busy working out a solution. "Okay, dear. Wait here. I'll be back."

My knight in navy blue casual slacks and a cream colored flight jacket headed out into the crowded terminal.

As I watched his back disappear, I worried. "What does he want to talk about? If something had happened to one of the children, he would have mentioned it right away—or even called."

"Dida you say someting?" A dark-haired man next to me spoke.

"What?" I flushed with embarrassment.

"'Cus I don' speaka da Inglish too good yet." His dark-brown eyes pleaded for understanding.

"Oh, I see!" I spoke loudly and nodded my head up and down to demonstrate my friendliness. "Have you just arrived in our country?" I raised my voice and gestured meaningfully.

"Wha'?" His bushy brows almost joined in concentration.

"Come here? Just now?" I waved my hands as though fanning my face.

"Hokay!" With one step, he had his arms around me.

"Wha . . . !" I tried to speak his language as well as I could, ". . . are you doing!"

For what seemed like an eternity, we danced around. I struggled to get free, while he held me firmly in his grasp.

"Martha!" John's voice sounded. As he hurried toward me, the man with the dark eyes held me close in a protective manner.

"Husband!" I gasped while I wriggled.

"Hus-pan?" His puzzled eyes glanced warily at John.

"Spouse!" I shouted.

"Space?" His hold softened.

"Amoray, uh, mate, uh . . ."

"Boss?" Relaxing his grip, he handed me to John. "You gotta take betta care a her. She got no shoes. Lease in my country we has shoes." Shaking his head, he melted into the crowd.

"John! Where have you been? I could have been mugged!" Holding a shoe in each hand, I stood trembling.

"Looks like you had it under control, Martha. Poor guy. Wonder if you're the first one he's met in our fair country?" He did, however, put his arm around my shoulder. "I couldn't find a wheelchair, so you'll be riding on a baggage cart."

By the time I'd ridden through the airport and out to the parking lot in abject humiliation, bruised a toe on a passer-by (who said some extremely unkind things), and been deposited on the passenger side of our car, my stomach cramped itself into a fit.

"All set, Martha?" John turned the key, and the car roared into traffic sounding like a souped-up stock car.

"What's wrong with the car, John?"

"Dropped the muffler on the way. I'll get it fixed tomorrow." Skillfully my husband steered us through traffic.

"Is that what you want to talk to me about?" I hollered above the noise.

"No." John changed lanes.

"Is it my car? Is my car all right?" I shouted.

"Your car's fine, Martha," John quietly replied. "You don't have to yell now. We're at a red light."

"Right," I commented. "When are you going to tell me?"

"Guess I'll find a place to pull over before we get home," my husband answered, staring at the car ahead.

My stomach leaped into a knot of pain.

When we arrived at a parking lot, I feared the worst.

John switched off the automobile engine.

"Well?" I couldn't restrain my mouth from jumping right in.

"Martha, I wanted to speak to you before we arrived home because—"

"Are the kids all right?" I broke in over his soft-spoken manner with a bit of hysteria.

"What?" He seemed to squirm in his seat. "Oh, yes, fine. No problems there. I would have phoned you."

"What is it then?" I began pawing through my purse, zipping and unzipping compartments.

"Lose something, Martha?"

"I think I might," I responded meaningfully.

"Oh." My husband began drumming his fingers on the car steering wheel. "Martha, there's someone at our house . . ."

My stomach sank out of sight. Visions of Andrea Gray blasted my brain apart. "John, I feel sick."

John forged ahead. "Glen Bobbin, you remember, my old college buddy, telephoned me while you were at your mother's. He'll be staying with us for a couple of weeks," John stated confidently. "I didn't think you'd mind."

"Mind?" Stunned, I sat still.

"I thought you'd like to know so you can set an extra place at supper tonight."

"Tonight?"

"Martha, do you feel all right? You're repeating yourself again." John started the car and pulled out into traffic.

"Oh, fine, John. I was just wondering what I'll fix for dinner. I haven't been home for a couple of weeks, so to have someone just sort of drop in and eat when I don't even know what is in the cupboards—"

"No problem, dear. Glen's already been here for a few days. He knows his way around." John turned down our street.

My eyebrows shot to my hairline. "You mean he's *already* staying at our house? Where is he sleeping?"

"On the sofa," John replied easily.

"Did you fold out the bed?"

"Nope." John turned into our driveway.

"*Nope?*" My voice squeaked. "You mean you didn't get out sheets and a blanket? He slept on the sofa cushions?"

"Relax, Martha. George found him an old blanket. He's fine."

"Well, it's not fine with me, John Christian. How could you do such a thing? You know I haven't been well, and I have to work extra hours now that I'm back, and—"

"Hey, buddy!" A deep baritone voice preceded an almost six-foot-tall masculine frame, topped by salt and pepper curly hair cut close to his well-shaped head.

"Glen!" John jumped out of the car and shook hands with a middle-aged man weighing about two hundred twenty-five pounds.

"I'll bet he's hungry too," I muttered under my breath.

"Glen, I'd like you to meet the little woman—the other half—the better side . . ."

Glaring at John with my eyes, smiling with my lips, I conveyed my displeasure to my spouse while sticking out my right hand to our guest. "Hello, Glen. It's a pleasure to meet you," I said.

"Ahh, Martha! A vision of loveliness in motion."

Instant dislike formed a cancer of resentment in my heart.

Ignoring his greeting, I addressed my husband, "John, will you carry in my suitcases, please? I need to freshen up before I prepare dinner."

"Hey, little lady!" Glen Bobbin's once bulging arm muscles flexed as he struggled to lift me up. "I'm treating tonight!"

Looking at him sideways out of the corner of my eye, I flushed with embarrassment. "That's very nice of you. Now, please let go of me." Hurrying into the house, I escaped the man I didn't like and the man of the house.

Quickly my eyes took in the condition of our home. "Disaster!" I put my hands on my hips and ran my eyes around the living room. "Not a single surface uncluttered!" Groaning, I began gathering newspapers, magazines, juice glasses, gum wrappers, and shoes. Then I picked cookie crumbs, lint, and rubber bands off the carpet. "They've been shooting at each other again," I complained, scooping up mounds of paper bits squeezed into little balls for ammunition.

Too tired to yell, I sat down on the sofa and leaned my head back. "I smell something," I mumbled to myself. Sniffing like a small puppy, I followed my nose around the couch. "A cigar! This Glen person smokes cigars! Well, he better not—"

"Hey, Martha!" Glen's voice boomed behind my back. "I've been looking all over for that! It's one of my best ones!" He chuckled heartily.

I held out the offending stogie. "Glad I could be of help."

"You never saw me when I was a football hero," he remarked, sitting down on the sofa as though he owned it.

"No, I never did," I answered, walking across the room. "Please excuse me. I need to get this place cleaned up before dinner."

"Ever think about selling your house, Martha?" The bomb dropped suddenly.

"Selling?" I stood with my mouth open, holding a sack of guinea pig food that George had neglected to return to its proper place in the supply closet.

As Glen Bobbin leaned back and put his arm on the sofa back, his suit coat fell open, exposing twenty pounds of extra flab circling his midriff. "John told me you repeat things a lot and not to worry about it. Yes, selling your house. I'm in real estate sales. John must have told you. He and I discussed a little deal where you might let this old place go and buy yourselves that hobby farm he's always talked about."

"John has always talked about buying a hobby farm?" Mentally I searched my brain trying to remember if John had *ever* in all our years mentioned a farm. "Well, he used to kid a lot about getting out of teaching and out into the wilds of Montana . . ." I frowned and scratched the back of my right hand. "He used to say something about chasing hogs or some such foolishness . . ."

"Well, Martha, his dreams are about to become *your reality*! But, hey! We can talk about that later. There's a game on TV I don't want to miss!" Removing his suit jacket, he draped it over my favorite Boston rocker, flipped the television on, and settled himself in a prone position on my couch. "Little hard on the neck here, Martha. You wouldn't happen to have a pillow, would you?"

Without a word I found a pillow. "Excuse me a moment, Glen, I want to speak to John." Plastering a phony smile on my face, I backed out of the room. I found my mate outside getting ready to mow the lawn.

Carefully I measured my words. "John! How could you!"

"Hi, honey," replied my spouse, unwinding the lawn mower cord. "Don't you think Glen is a great guy? He hopes to purchase a large section of land in Arizona and develop it into low-cost housing for the poor."

"Using who's money?"

John considered my mood before answering. "Martha, I meant to tell you about a little deal Glen talked to me about—"

"Glen just did." I clipped the words. "Are you getting out of teaching?"

Slowly John let the lawn mower cord drop to the ground. "You know I've talked about it from time to time, Martha."

"You haven't talked to *me* for a long time, John." I crossed my arms across my chest and stood ready for battle.

"Maybe it's time for a change," he replied quietly.

"You mean you've already made up your mind." I began to

pace back and forth on the grass. "How much does a hobby farm cost? Will it take our life savings?"

"Yes." His one-word answer twisted my stomachache into a tight knot. "John, I know you. When you give a one-word answer, that means there's no discussion." Angry tears filled my eyes. "I just don't know how you could do this without telling me."

My mate for life turned away from me to tinker with the lawn mower. "This thing's not working right," he said.

My chest tightened. "What does *Andrea* think?"

John flipped the switch on the lawn mower. I watched it leap into life.

I'd said too much.

Despair enveloped me. Knowing I'd put my foot in my mouth, I turned on my heel and hurried to the safety of the basement laundry room. "Why does the world walk on me?" I threw some old towels in the washing machine and watched the hot water pour in. "Everybody else has important decisions to make. I, on the other hand, stand in the wings and watch the stage show. When William Shakespeare said, 'All the world's a stage,' he didn't write in a part for Martha Christian." Dumping detergent into the washer, I stared hard at the bubbles as they foamed over and covered the dirty laundry. "I'd like a little recognition from my family and other people I know." The machine began to chug. "How do I get it?"

Pacing around the basement floor, I peered through the window and watched John mow up and down in even rows. "Why do I try to be noticed by being nice? Maybe Andrea Gray has the answer, after all. She pushes people around, and they not only listen, they applaud her efforts!" With my toe I pushed at a piece of gray dust that rolled aimlessly across the floor.

"Ma?"

"Ginny!" I jumped back with the small shriek. "How did you get in here?"

"I walked in. Mr. Christian said I could. He said you were in here." She popped her gum nervously.

"Oh, I didn't see you out there."

"Yeah, well, [snap, crack] I was there. Now, I'm here." She

fiddled with her frizzy blond hair.

"Come on in and sit down, Ginny," I said with a smile.

"Okay," she agreed, "but I'm already here."

"Ginny, Eleanor Roosevelt said, 'No one can make you feel inferior without your consent.' " I shared my non sequitur information.

"That's good, Ma," she agreed, pulling over an old chair. "I like it." She sat down. "What does it mean?"

"It means, Ginny, my dear, that God helps only those who help themselves. Come on upstairs for coffee." I smiled gregariously.

"Oh, I get it [popple, crack]. I'm not supposed to be a wimp—"

"That's *wimple*, Ginny," I corrected, leading the way to the kitchen.

"Wimple?" Her gum-chewing slowed to a stop.

"Yes," I replied confidently, putting water on the stove to boil.

"Ma." Ginny's sparkling dark-brown eyes grew serious. "You've got something wrong here! There's no such word as *wimple*."

Whizzing past her to the bookcase, I whipped open the dictionary. "Here it is, right here." I ran my fingers down the page. "Whim, whimper, whimsical, whimsy, whine, whip . . . That's strange." I tapped my fingers on the printed page. "I wonder how you spell *wimple*."

"W-i-m-p," spelled Ginny.

"Of course. I knew that," I responded, flipping the pages backward, then forward. "Here it is: 'wimple, a nun's head covering so arranged as to leave only the face exposed.' Hmm." Scrunching my eyes, I looked again.

"Where's *wimp*?" Ginny grabbed the dictionary. "Here it is, Ma. *Wimp*, a weak or something person." She slapped the book shut.

"Or something?" Pouring boiling water into two cups, I set instant coffee and whitener on the table.

"I couldn't figure out the other word, but I'm sure it meant more of the same." Reaching into her purse, she found another piece of gum, unwrapped it, and popped it into her mouth in addition to the other one.

"Ginny, if you don't mind, I think I'd like to be alone right now." I wiped my perspiring brow with the back of my right hand.

"Sure, Ma," she replied sympathetically. "It's pretty hot today. You want to watch it at your age. You could get heat stroke or something." She pulled the chewing gum out of her mouth and folded it in a paper napkin. "Something I came to tell you, though." Ginny fiddled with her coffee cup, rattling it in the saucer. "There's some money missing at work, and maybe some stock, too. You know, like lipstick and cosmetics and candy."

My stomach cramped hard, and nausea swept through my system. "What are you trying to tell me, Ginny?" My hazel eyes searched Ginny's brown ones for clues.

Her troubled glance told me I was the one in trouble. "Drulene says . . ." Pools of tears shimmered, then spilled softly down her cheeks.

"Says. Yes, says . . ." I prompted while handing her a facial tissue.

" . . . says you took the money to cover up how much you spent on the renovations so Mr. Kleaver wouldn't fire you!" The words rushed out and stabbed me repeatedly.

"Fire me?" I sat down quickly on the chair across the table from Ginny and held on to my stomach. "Don't be ridiculous, Ginny. You know Mr. Kleaver wouldn't fire me. It's out of the question! He would never take Drulene's word over mine, Ginny. You're worrying needlessly."

"Oh, Ma, it's all my fault!" Ginny sobbed into three tissues at once. "I was afraid of that Mrs. Gray lady. I knew Drulene was her niece because that's how she got the job . . ." Ginny buried her nose into the damp tissues and grabbed three more.

"There, there, Ginny," I soothed, smoothing back her stiff blond hair.

"Drulene always said if I gave her any trouble, she'd get you to fire me. Oh, Ma, I'm so sorry." Ginny's shoulders heaved as she gulped in air to continue. "I saw Drulene take cash from your cash drawer when she took over for you . . ."

Instantly I remembered allowing Drulene to count my cash because she pressured me to let her help. Numb, blind fear lashed into my being. I was guilty too because I knew better. I also was afraid of Andrea Gray.

Ginny turned her tear-streaked face toward me. "What are we going to do, Ma?"

Standing next to Ginny, listening to her cry, I also remembered Andrea Gray's power to hurt. When Ginny had called the police about the three carts Andrea wanted, Andrea called the Chief of Police and simply took the carts. It was a case of what Andrea Gray wanted, Andrea Gray got.

The telephone rang and we both jumped. "Hello?" I answered as cheerily as possible with a noose waiting to be looped over my neck.

"Hi, Martha," Jean, my best friend of the ages, began, "I wanted to share some great news."

"You're buying a new house," I commented without interest.

"I'm joining Andrea Gray's country club."

"But, Jean, you don't even like golf!" Aching took over where my heart should have been. My husband, my position at work, and now my best friend all seemed to fall into the domain of the great Andrea Gray.

"You don't sound very thrilled at the idea, Martha. I would have thought you would be happy for me." Jean's hurt came through loud and clear.

Just then I heard Joe yelling from the basement. "Mom! Mom!"

"Excuse me, Jean, I have to hang up. I hear Joe calling me."

"Andrea was right, Martha. She said you wouldn't be happy about this." The cut went deep.

"Goodbye, Jean." Hanging up the receiver, I turned my back on the best friend I'd ever had.

"Mom! Mom!" Joe's voice boomed into my brain while his body emerged into the kitchen. "Glen Bobbin says he'll give me driving lessons in his car! Dad says I can. Can I?"

Lifting my sad eyes to greet his jubilant face I replied, "Joe, do you know what a rhetorical question is?"

His blank expression answered my inquiry.

"*When* are you going?" I asked mechanically.

"We're going to get my learner's permit right now, and then I get to start!" Rubbing his hands together in glee, he danced around the kitchen like a two-year-old.

"Would you like to say hello to Ginny?" I knew when I was whipped.

"Sure, Mom! Hi, Ginny. Bye, Ginny." And he vanished.

Meanwhile, Ginny freshened her face and popped new gum into her mouth. Her composure returned. "What do you think we can do then, Mrs. Christian?" Her jaws moved up and down in steady motion.

"Do?" I rubbed my eyebrows with my thumbs. "Ginny, I believe I have to think about all this for a little bit."

Flashing a huge smile, Ginny threw her arms around me and gave me a hug. "I'm so glad I told you, Ma! I feel so much better now!"

"Me too," I replied lamely.

Once alone, I took out a piece of paper and pen. "I know Deborah faced a great battle with Sisera. He ' . . . gathered together his nine hundred iron chariots and all the men with him, from Harosheth Haggoyim to the Kishon River.'[40] So, for Deborah to have to march against a line like that, she must have felt a little nervous."

Tapping my fingers nervously on the blank paper, I wondered how to begin. "I guess I should list some pros and cons. People always say that helps."

I sat and stared at a blank wall for a while. "Pros and cons of what?" Feeling like I was fighting phantoms, I prayed, "Lord, help, please."

The Quiet Voice replied, "The Lord is my shepherd; I shall not want. He maketh me to lie down in green pastures; he leadeth me beside the still waters. He restoreth my soul: he leadeth me in the paths of righteousness for his name's sake. Yea, though I walk through the valley of the shadow of death, I will fear no evil; for thou art with me; thy rod and thy staff they comfort me. Thou preparest a table before me in the presence of mine enemies; thou anointest my head with oil; my cup runneth over. Surely goodness and mercy shall follow me all the days of my life: and I will dwell in the house of the Lord for ever."[41]

Picking up my pen, I wrote the following:

FEAR	FAITH

1. What do I fear?
   a. Andrea Gray
   b. moving to Montana
   c. financial reverses
   d. other people's negative opinions
   e. death
	1. What does the Bible say?
	   "So have no fear of them; for nothing is concealed that will not be revealed, or kept secret that will not become known."[42]

2. Where does this fear originate?
   a. the world
   b. the flesh (me)
   c. the devil
	2. Jesus said, "Don't be frightened!"[43]

3. What can I do?	

Just as I thought, *I should get on the other side of this list,* a window-rattling crash resounded through the house. Racing down the stairs, I reached the back door as a white-faced Glen Bobbin burst into our basement.

"Where's Joe?" Charging past him, I ran outside.

"Mom!" Joe sat huddled over the steering wheel of Glen's car, the door of which was imbedded in the side of our house.

"Joe!" Shoving myself around the twisted car door, I felt my son's face for injuries. "Joe," I murmured to him as I had when he was a baby, "are you hurt?"

My middle son shook his head from side to side. "It was bad, Mom." He convulsed into tears.

"Come on, Joe." I tugged at his left arm. "Let's go into the house. How about a bottle of pop? Would you like that?"

Joe allowed himself to be led into the house, refused my offer of cookies, and retreated to his room to lie down.

Then I went hunting for Glen Bobbin. I found him outside in the carport, staring at his crumpled car door. "How did this happen, Glen?" My dislike of this arrogant man grew as I glared into his proud eyes.

"Joe's a little shaken, Martha. These things happen." Shrugging his shoulders, my unwanted guest walked around his mangled automobile.

"What things, Glen?" My question demanded his attention.

"Okay." Glen Bobbin walked around and leaned against the back fender of his car, facing me. "Joe hit a dog on the way home. He was so scared he overshot your driveway and drove right through your carport and into your backyard. When he tried to back up into the carport, he opened the car door to see where he was going. My guess is he stepped on the gas pedal too hard. Anyway, the car leaped back and jammed the door into the side of your house." Glen rubbed his hand together to wipe off car grease. "Got a rag, Martha?"

Fury rose inside me. Too stunned to answer, I clenched my fists. I had one thought, one person who deserved the blame for my son's pain.

John.

12 / Prophetess

"Hear this, you kings! Listen, you rulers! I will sing to the Lord, I will sing; I will make music to the Lord, the God of Israel."[44]

I stared in disbelief at my balding boss, Mr. Kleaver. "Do you mean you're *firing* me?" My hands shook noticeably as I stood before the desk I had occupied as temporary manager of Kleaver's Meats and Merchandise.

My employer shifted uncomfortably in the soft desk chair I had twirled around in during my managing days. "You understand, Martha, with Len here now, and me back to work full time, and the economy a little slow . . ."

The supermarket smells seemed to collect before my eyes while my feet slipped out from under me.

"Ma?" Ginny's voice broke through the clouds of unknowing that swallowed my consciousness.

Cold water dripped down my forehead. I struggled to see who washed my face. "Ginny?" My vision cleared, and I looked into brown eyes surrounded by frizzed-blond hair.

"You fainted, Martha," announced my previous employer, Mr. Kleaver. "You sure scared me!" He wiped his sweating brow with a white handkerchief. "Yes, ma'am." He tucked the white flag into his back pants' pocket out of sight. "I even had chest pains over that one!"

Sitting up, embarrassment of classic proportions flooded over me.

"Thank you, Ginny," Mr. Kleaver pronounced over his half-glasses. "You can go back to work now. Martha will be fine; won't you, Martha?"

"Oh yes, fine, of course fine," I parroted, pulling myself up and onto a straight-backed chair. "Let me catch my breath. It must have been something I ate."

"As I was saying, Martha." My ex-boss shuffled some papers on top of *his* desk. "You can see my point, now that I am back."

Unable to see anything but disappointment, disuse, and public disgrace ahead of me, I replied, "Certainly, Mr. Kleaver. I'll clean out my, uh, your desk right away."

"No need, Martha," he responded without looking at me; "your belongings have been placed in a paper bag and tagged with your name on them."

"What?" Unable to believe my own hearing, I mechanically glanced over and saw a sack in the corner marked "Martha Christian." "Oh, yes, thank you." Struggling to stand without falling over, I covered the few steps to the corner while my heart pounded out a funeral dirge.

My previous boss, the man I'd possibly saved from death, casually leaned across his desk and extended his hand. "It's been a pleasure working with you, Martha. Ginny has your final paycheck."

"Oh yes, thank you," I replied, while nails drove into my spirit. "Yes, I'll do that."

Somehow I stumbled through the store. Feeling every eye upon me, I made my way shamefaced to Ginny's checkout lane. Then I stood and waited like any other customer for her to serve me.

"Thank you very much, sir," she recited to a faceless man. Quickly she put up her CLOSED sign. "Oh, Ma." Her voice resounded with the sympathy of the ages for the discarded ones in life.

"It's okay, Ginny," I whispered, fighting my feelings of uselessness; "just give me the check."

Without another word, my best ex-checker rang out her machine and handed me my check.

"See ya," I said.

I walked two blocks before I realized I'd driven my own automobile to work. Turning around hastily, I jumped when a small dog leaped out from behind a tiny fence and barked furiously at me.

By the time I made it back and sat behind the wheel of my car, my stomach burned in pain. The air felt too tight in my throat and I struggled for control. "What will I do?"

Almost before I knew it, I had driven myself to a public telephone. I watched my right hand tap out the number so familiar. Waiting, I listened to the telephone ring in Oregon. "Mom?"

"Martha, what is it?"

The dam burst as tears flooded down my cheeks. "Mom, you've got to help me. Oh, Mom . . ." I couldn't speak for a moment. "Mom, I'm okay, I really am, but I've been fired." A salty drop drizzled down the right side of my nose and waited to fall to the ground below.

"Where are you?" My practical mother questioned me as gently as she would a small child.

"In a phone booth," I sniffled.

"Where is John?"

"John?" Remembering my anger at John because of Andrea Gray, Glen Bobbin, moving to Montana, and life in general, I shot back, "John is probably moving to Montana without me, Mother."

"Are you hurt?" Her soft tone probed my problems.

"Hurt?" I rubbed my forehead. "No, I'm not hurt, Mom—not physically anyway." I blew my nose on a clean, white hanky, while I felt my heart lighten. My mother represented hope—"Anxious hearts are very heavy but a word of encouragement does wonders!"[45]

"Martha, listen to me for a moment, will you?"

"Yes," I replied, perking up my ears.

"A wise woman builds her house, while a foolish woman tears hers down by her own efforts."[46]

"Andrea Gray is ripping my house apart, Mom," I answered full of self-pity.

"What are you prepared to do about it?"

Her question stumped me. Rubbing my right eye with the fingers of my right hand, I stared out the telephone booth glass and noticed the sun streaming through summer-green trees. "Do?"

"Martha, forgive me, dear, but I found a small notebook lying in your room at home with notations you made while visiting me. I've taken the liberty of mailing it to you. I couldn't help peeking inside to see if it was important. You had written about your friend Deborah, remember?"

"Yes, Mom, I remember, and you've helped me more than you know!"

"I believe in you, Martha." Mother cleared her throat. "Now solve this mess." Her reprimand straightened my spine.

"Thanks, Mom. I will."

Hurrying home, I was glad when an empty house greeted me. With a light step, I quickly mounted the basement stairs and ran back to our bedroom. On the night table lay my Bible. As precious as gold, God's Word waited to comfort me, strengthen me, and straighten my thinking.

"Let God train you, for he is doing what any loving father does for his children. Whoever heard of a son who was never corrected? If God doesn't punish you when you need it, as other fathers punish their sons, then it means that you aren't really God's son at all—that you don't really belong in his family. Since we respect our fathers here on earth, though they punish us, should we not all the more cheerfully submit to God's training so that we can begin really to live?

"Our earthly fathers trained us for a few brief years, doing the best for us that they knew how, but God's correction is always right and for our best good, that we may share his holiness. Being punished isn't enjoyable while it is happening—it hurts! But afterwards we can see the result, a quiet growth in grace and character.

"So take a new grip with your tired hands, stand firm on your shaky legs, and mark out a straight, smooth path for your feet so that those who follow you, though weak and lame, will not fall and hurt themselves, but become strong.

"Try to stay out of all quarrels—"[47]

"Excuse, me, Lord," I prayed, "but I don't think you've met Andrea Gray," I interjected.

"—and seek to live a clean and holy life, for one who is not holy will not see the Lord."[48]

Reverently, I closed the Living Word. Changing my clothes quickly, I hurried to the front door to check the mail. There, on the rug, lay a brown envelope bearing Mother's familiar script.

"Thanks, Mom," I whispered, ripping open the envelope.

Inside the cover of my notebook, Mom had carefully placed a pressed purple pansy—my favorite. Attached to the stem, a tiny slip of paper read: "I love you."

"I love you too, Mom," I said to the empty air, "and I'm going to learn to do this thing beginning with right now."

The mantel clock chimed two as I sat down on the living room sofa and opened my notebook.

You will need more than your notebook. The Comforter breathed counsel into my soul.

Excitement born of hope lifted me to my feet. Hunting around, I found my Bible, a dictionary of biblical terms, a concordance, and a collegiate dictionary. Settling down on the sofa, I opened the Bible first and read, "Now Deborah, a prophetess . . ."

"That's strange. I never noticed the word *prophetess* before. That's female for prophet. Wonder what that means?"

Fifteen minutes later, I'd learned a prophet spoke for God and had above average moral and divine inspiration. Back in the Bible I found: ". . . and when the Spirit rested upon them, they prophesied [sounding forth the praises of God and declaring His will]."[49]

"Sounding out the praises of God," I repeated out loud. "I've been so mad at Andrea Gray I haven't been glad about God!"

"Deborah . . . judged Israel at that time."[50]

"What does a judge need to judge?" I asked myself.

Wisdom, The Quiet One responded deep in my soul.

"If any of you lack wisdom, let him ask of God, that giveth to all . . . but . . . ask in faith, nothing wavering. . . ."[51]

The clock sounded out the half hour. "The first thing I'm

doing is throwing away Ginny's notes on being assertive." My heart lightened as I hurried to the linen closet.

Feeling around under the stacks of clean sheets, my fingers ran across crumpled paper. "Ah, ha! Here they are."

Pulling them out, I commented, "I don't think this is doing Ginny one bit of good or she would have defended me against Drulene's false charges of stealing. Therefore"—I ripped as I walked to the kitchen—"off to the trash can they go!" Stuffing the paper shreds under a deteriorating banana peel, I turned my back on the wastebasket and strode resolutely back to the living room couch.

In my notes on Deborah, I discovered some things I must do to rectify my situation. First, be willing to face Andrea Gray.

Chills of terror swept up my spine, reached my neck, and shot electric currents of fear along my scalp.

Taking a deep breath, I wrote this down. "Faith overcomes fear—see Andrea Gray this week."

The clock chimed three. "Only an hour before the kids hit the door," I advised. "Quickly, quickly! What else must I do?"

"Face them honestly," a Quiet Voice seemed to say.

"How?" Tears filled my eyes as I recalled my anger at John for planning a move to Montana without me; my mad, hurt feelings at Jean for deserting me to join Andrea's country club; my rage at Glen Bobbin for allowing Joe to hit a dog, keep driving, and crash a car door into our house; my frustration with my strong-willed sons who made up their minds without consulting me; and my self-pity at losing my job—probably because of Andrea Gray's niece, Drulene. "Most of all, Lord, I am allowing myself to try to use the devil's weapons to bring down the devil's strongholds."

Bowing my head, I sat silently, waiting.

Opening my Bible, I read, "Since you have been chosen by God who has given you this new kind of life, and because of his deep love and concern for you, you should practice tender-hearted mercy and kindness to others. Don't worry about making a good impression on them but be ready to suffer quietly and patiently. Be gentle and ready to forgive; never hold grudges. Remember, the Lord forgave you, so you must forgive others."[52]

By the time the clock gonged 3:30 in the afternoon, I'd prayed my armor on and taken up the sword of the Spirit.[53] Peace settled my soul.

By the time George arrived home at 4:00 P.M., I had a cake in the oven and the following verse copied and stuck on the refrigerator door. "For Thou has girded me with strength for battle; Thou hast subdued under me those who rose up against me."[54]

"Something smells good, Mom!" George sniffed the air.

"How was day camp?" I handed him a glass of milk and a double-fudge chocolate cookie.

"Okay," he responded, flopping down on a kitchen chair. "How come you're home?

His question hit like a bullet to the brain. How could I tell him I'd been fired?

The Quiet One enabled me to pick up my sword: *"Instead, we will lovingly follow the truth at all times—speaking truly, dealing truly, living truly—and so become more and more in every way like Christ who is the Head of his body, the church."*[55]

"I was fired, George."

"Wow, Mom! That's too bad. It's probably because of that money you spent." He bit his cookie in two and examined the middle.

"Money I spent?" I raised my eyebrows in shock.

"Yeah. Drulene told me you bought a new roof, ten smoke alarms, a park for in front of the store, and built a special house just for people to rest while they're washing their hands."

"George, I would like you to find out from the source—not listen to gossip."

"What does that mean?" He shoved his glasses up on his nose.

"It means you should ask me instead of making up your mind without facts."

"Okay, what happened?" He stuck out his hand for another cookie.

"I'm not certain, George, but I think Drulene may have had something to do with it." I handed him two cookies—one for each hand.

"Uh oh, that means Mrs. Gray is gonna get you."

"George, it doesn't mean anything like that. In fact, in the morning I'm going to bake my best lemon meringue pie and take it over to her."

My youngest son studied me. "You okay, Mom?"

"Never better. Here's a carrot for Ben."

"Sure, Mom." George stuffed the cookies in his mouth, took the carrot, and departed.

When J.J. came home from a hard day delivering ice cream, I faced him. "John Jr., I want you to know that I was fired today." Taking a deep breath, I waited for the storm to hit.

J.J.'s blue eyes covered my face. "Well, Mom, you can always get another job." He frowned. "Can't you?"

"I guess I can. How was your day?"

"Fine. Babs is moving back next week. Did I tell you?"

"No, I didn't know."

"You've been pretty busy, Mom." J.J. patted me on the shoulder. "It's all set, but I don't know what I'm going to do, though." My oldest son rummaged through the fridge.

"Do?" I sat down on the step stool and waited.

"Yeah, Mom. I've been accepted to three universities." Grabbing a piece of cheese and an apple, he leaned against the kitchen counter. "One on the east coast, one in Alaska, and one about a hundred miles from here."

"Oh," I responded weakly. "I see."

"Yeah, so if Babs is here, I don't want to be *there*, if you know what I mean."

I began peeling potatoes. "I'll pray for your wisdom, John."

"You never called me John before. I like it! Thanks, Mom. I'll let you know what happens." Kissing me on the cheek, he departed.

Just as I turned the chicken in the frying pan, Joe appeared at my elbow.

"Hi, Mom."

"Hi," I replied, "what's new?"

"Not much." He hung around the room shuffling his feet.

"Hungry?"

"Not much."

"How about a hug from your aging mother?"

"Okay."

Reaching my arms around my middle son, I noticed he stood taller. "You're getting taller, Joe."

His brown eyes twinkled. "You're getting shorter!" He pulled himself up to his full height.

Standing back, I still held his hands. "Joe, how do you feel about driving my car?"

My son's head dipped down suddenly. "Gotta tie my shoe," he commented.

"Did you hear me, Joe? Would you like to drive my car?"

"Who's going with me?" he replied from a stooped position.

"Well, I guess I could, or your dad—"

"Does Dad know I killed a dog?"

"Did you tell him?"

"No."

"I didn't either."

Joe stood up and opened the refrigerator door. "So I guess Glen Bobbin didn't tell him."

It occurred to me that our family life had fragmented to polite courtesy while I'd waged my war against Andy. "I'll talk to him tonight, honey. I'm certain he will understand."

"What if he gets mad?"

"What if he does? We still have to face truth, don't we?"

"I guess so." Joe departed with relief etched across his fifteen-year-old face.

During supper, Glen Bobbin ate with gusto. "Pass me some more of those great mashed potatoes of yours, Martha!" Glen stuck out his hands.

Refusing to take offense, I passed the potatoes while placing a pleasant expression on my face.

"Excellent chicken, Martha," John commented. "How did you have time to make this after a busy day at Kleaver's?"

"I was fired today," I responded, passing the southern fried chicken to George.

"How's your stomach, Martha?" John's sky-blue eyes said many things in the glance that followed—all of them supportive.

"Fine," I responded honestly across the faces of my children and Glen Bobbin.

His blue eyes gleamed with a light of old. "Think I'll have some more of that delicious chicken myself, George. Now that your mom has been sacked we'll get some mighty good meals around here again." He winked at Joe.

Startled into quietude by the sudden rapport between their parents, our sons ate their dinner politely, pleasantly, and peacefully.

Later that evening, I talked privately with my husband. "John, did you know that Joe was the one who ran Glen's car door into the side of our house?"

"Joe?" He walked over and closed our bedroom door. "No, I thought Glen did it. I hated to ask him. What happened?"

After I related the details, I concluded with, "I wish Glen would leave."

"Martha, I'm sorry. I noticed the situation going from bad to worse, but, truthfully," he smoothed back his thinning hair, "I didn't want to take on Glen." John sat down on the edge of the bed. "I guess I never told you, Martha, but Glen was the kind of guy I never felt I could be—you know, football hero, semi-pro ball after college, the girls waited in line to date him—that kind of thing."

"John, I never knew that! All these years married, and you never told me." Realizing the injustice I'd done to my mate, I went over and put my arms around him.

"It's no big deal," he replied, squirming uncomfortably at my show of sympathy.

Unabashed, I kissed him on top of his balding head. "John, I have a confession to make." Tears filled my eyes.

"You didn't take the money from Kleaver's." He took my cold hand in his two warm ones.

"How did you—"

"Andy told me. Apparently Drulene has been stealing bits of money from your cash drawer. Len caught her once or twice. Today he called Andy. Andy called me to see what I thought she should do."

Fighting down my resentment, I faced the situation with

truth on my tongue. "John, why does Andrea call you? Why doesn't she ask her own husband, Leonard?" I stood up and began to pace back and forth across the room. "In fact, I've never seen Leonard at church. Frankly, John, I don't like it."

"Little jealous, eh, wife?" John chuckled good-naturedly. "I *am* pretty irresistible."

"This is no time for jokes," I stated firmly. "I'm going to bake my best lemon meringue pie tomorrow morning and face the music with Andrea. This strife between her and me has gone on long enough."

"Does she know you're coming?" John's tone changed.

"I'm calling her this evening." If I had looked at my husband at that point, I would have been prepared for what was ahead, but I didn't. "John, are we moving to Montana?" My bluntness caught him off guard.

"Now that you've lost your job we might as well," he quipped with a smile on his face.

"I asked you not to joke, John." I crossed my arms and waited. "I should have told you, but I didn't. I was too mad at Andrea Gray for trying to steal my husband. Anyway, I don't want to move. I'm sorry I got angry instead of telling you that." My heart hammered, but I continued. "John, I would like to feel close to you again."

He held his arms out to me. "Me too. And, no, we won't go. Maybe when the kids are grown and gone, if you'd like that too."

"Really? You don't mind?" I stood very still, watching his eyes, the face I loved.

"Really."

The telephone rang just as I nestled into John's arms.

John reached over to the night table and answered the clang. "Hello?" John winked at me. "Hi, Andy, glad to hear from you. I think Martha wants to talk to you . . ."

My husband held out the receiver.

Taking a deep breath, I spoke into the telephone. "Andrea, I'd like to visit you tomorrow, and I'd like to bring a little gift."

The silence at the other end told me I was on the right track.

"Will that be all right, Andrea?"

"Very well, Martha. What time?" Her voice registered no emotion.

"Early afternoon, if that's suitable," I replied.

"I'll see you then, Martha." Andrea Gray hung up her end of the conversation.

I handed John the receiver.

"I'm impressed!" My mate's blue eyes reflected admiration.

"John, I've learned that 'wisdom is better than weapons of war,'[56] and 'wisdom is mightier than strength.' "[57]

"Martha," John's eyes turned serious, "I'll take Joe out to drive, and I'll talk to him. He'll be fine."

"Thank you."

"And, Glen will be gone when you return tomorrow." His face set, I knew he would see it through.

"Want to go for a moonlight stroll?" I flirted like a young girl.

"With you?" He gave me a quick squeeze. "You're on."

The August air had cooled as we stepped outside. As we walked past the O's house, I said excitedly, "John, look! There's a FOR SALE sign on the lawn!"

"That went up yesterday, Martha," my spouse said simply.

Craning my neck, I spied Mrs. O bent down under her front shrubs. "Yoo-hoo!" I waved my hand to catch her attention.

"We're moving!" she hollered back.

"John!" I tugged on his sleeve. "She spoke! Let's go talk to her."

"Better quit while you're ahead, Martha," John responded, pulling me along. "Didn't you come out tonight to stroll with me?" His clear blue eyes twinkled.

"You're right, I did," I agreed, putting my hand through his arm.

The next morning, while I waited for the pie to finish baking, the summer heat felt like a hot breath across the land. Taking out my notebook, I wrote, "True assertion is a confidence born of trusting God."

On the way to Andrea's house, I prayed, "Thank you, Lord, for going ahead of me. I know 'it is better to take refuge in the Lord than to trust in man.' "[58]

Fear receded.

Taking a deep breath, and trying to remember not to fear, I rang the doorbell of Andrea Gray's house while balancing my perfect lemon meringue pie.

The door opened. Inside stood the woman I'd feared, disliked, and struggled to overcome.

Trying to smile, I stuck out the pie.

"Come in, Martha," she said.

As I walked into the house, I noticed a shadowy figure silhouetted against their living room window. My eyebrows raised instinctively.

Andrea Gray caught my glance. "That's Leonard, Martha. He has muscular dystrophy. He won't know you're here. His muscles are wasting away. He spends his days as you see him—in a wheelchair."

Suddenly I saw Andrea Gray as she really was—dying husband and no children to comfort her in her old age. "Are you afraid?"

"Your husband has been a great help. Jean, too, of course." Her stiffness came from suffering.

Jealousy and anger faded as I began to comprehend the reality of her situation. "Andrea, I am sorry."

"Andy," she corrected. "I've taken care of the situation with Drulene. She will face the necessary charges. Mr. Kleaver will be calling you to offer you a position at his place of business." Andrea Gray placed my pie on her clean-as-a-whistle kitchen counter.

"Would you like to try a piece of my pie?"

"I would be most grateful, Martha." Her dark eyes shone with tears.

"Can I be your friend?" I countered, swallowing hard.

"You *may* if you *can*," she corrected, cutting two wedges of pie.

Digging in my purse, I pulled out a piece of crumpled paper. "This is from my notebook. A special lady taught me this recently." Hands trembling from emotion, I read out loud to Andrea Gray, "'For Thou hast been my help, and in the shadow of Thy wings I sing for joy.'"[59]

Notes

CHAPTER 1

1. Judges 4:4, KJV

CHAPTER 2

2. Judges 5:12, NASB
3. Judges 5:12–13, NASB
4. Judges 4:4, NASB

CHAPTER 3

5. Judges 4:5, NASB
6. *Today's Dictionary of the Bible*. Compiled by T. A. Bryant, Minneapolis: Bethany House Publishers, 1982, p. 6
7. Judges 4:4–6, NASB
8. *The New Bible Dictionary*. Organizing Editor, J. D. Douglas. Grand Rapids: Wm. B. Eerdman's Publishing Company, 1962, p. 133 (author's paraphrase)
9. Hebrews 11:32–34, NIV

CHAPTER 4

10. Judges 5:2, TLB
11. Judges 5:2–7, TLB
12. Judges 12:7, KJV
13. Judges 11:32, KJV
14. Judges 11:30–31, NIV

CHAPTER 5

15. Judges 5:7, NIV

16. Judges 5:7, NIV

CHAPTER 6

17. Judges 5:20, AMP
18. Hebrews 10:25, TLB
19. Luke 6:27–28, TLB
20. Judges 4:2–3, TLB

CHAPTER 7

21. Judges 4:18, NASB
22. Judges 4:18–19, NASB
23. James 3:15, TLB
24. Judges 4:21, NASB
25. Psalm 37:8, KJV

CHAPTER 8

26. Judges 5:8, NASB
27. Proverbs 18:24, NASB
28. Judges 4;8, NASB
29. Ephesians 4:32, NASB

CHAPTER 9

30. Judges 4:8, NIV
31. Psalm 55:21, KJV
32. Psalm 55:22, KJV

CHAPTER 10

33. Judges 5:21, NASB
34. Psalm 118:1–5, 7, 9, NIV
35. Judges 5:1–2, NIV
36. Judges 5:3, NIV
37. Based on Judges 5:5–15, NIV
38. Judges 5:21, NASB

CHAPTER 11

39. Judges 4:13, NIV
40. Judges 4:13, NIV
41. Psalm 23, KJV
42. Matthew 10:26, AMP
43. Matthew 28:10, TLB

CHAPTER 12

44. Judges 5:3, NIV
45. Proverbs 12:25, TLB
46. Proverbs 14:1, TLB
47. Hebrews 12:7–14, TLB
48. Hebrews 12:14, TLB
49. Numbers 11:25, AMP
50. Judges 4:4, KJV
51. James 1:5–6, KJV
52. Colossians 3:12–13, TLB
53. Ephesians 6:10–18, KJV
54. Psalm 18:39, NASB
55. Ephesians 4:15, TLB
56. Proverbs 21:14, TLB
57. Ecclesiastes 9:18, KJV
58. Proverbs 24:5, TLB
59. Psalm 118:8, NASB